Rage Revelry and Romance

Rage Revelry and Romance

Uday Prakash

Translated by
Robert A. Hueckstedt

YATRA
BOOKS
An imprint of Vani Prakashan Group

vaniprakashan.com

Paperback First Edition : 2024

Yatra Books is an imprint of Vani Prakashan Group

Head Office

4695, 21-A, Daryaganj, New Delhi 110 002, India
Phone : +91 11 23273167, 23275710

Registered Bookstores and Offices

Ashok Rajpath, Patna-800 004, Bihar
Coffee House Campus, Mahatma Gandhi Marg, Prayagraj-211 001, Uttar Pradesh
Mahatma Gandhi International Hindi University, Wardha-442 001, Maharashtra
36-A, Shakespeare Sarani, Near Rani Birla Girls College, Kolkata-700017, West Bengal

sales@vaniprakashan.in
vaniprakashan@gmail.com

Rage Revelry and Romance
by Uday Prakash
Translated by Robert A. Hueckstedt

ISBN : 978-93-90678-95-2
Fiction

Price : ₹ 325

Printed and bound in India at City Press, Delhi-110 095

Vani Prakashan's signature motif is created by Artist Maqbool Fida Husain

Contents

The Storyteller's Timepiece: Timelessness of Uday Prakash's Literary Oeuvre

The thirteen stories in this collection were first published in Hindi between 1982 and 1997. During most of that time, and since, Uday Prakash has been appraised by his peers and contemporaries as one of Hindi's best short story writers.

Uday Prakash considers himself, however, more a poet than a prose author. In addition to the more than thirty short stories he has written, he has also published three collections of poetry. It is the combination of his poetic sensibility to word choice and phrasing and his seemingly innate gift for creating a marvelous story that make his short stories so rich and memorable.

Uday Prakash was born in 1951 and raised near the Son River in a tribal area of the Chhattisgarh region of Madhya Pradesh. His father was of the Baghel caste, and his family has been one of the area's major landowners. The tribals treated his father as if he were their chief. When Uday Prakash was thirteen years old, his mother died; when he was eighteen, his father died. Both were victims of cancer.

In his late teens and early twenties Uday Prakash was an active member of the Communist Party of India, founding its student wing in Shahdol District. When Indira Gandhi proclaimed the Emergency in 1975, Uday Prakash was a post-MA student at Sagar University (Now Dr. Hari Singh Gour University), Sagar in Madhya Pradesh, and he had already applied for a position as Research Scholar at Jawaharlal Nehru University. Since he was a locally prominent member of the

CPI, and since the Government of India harassed and arrested rural grass roots workers of the CPI, Uday Prakash soon felt himself forced to leave Chhattisgarh for the anonymity of Delhi. He was accepted into JNU, and he lived in Delhi from 1975 to 1978. From 1978-1980 he taught at JNU's Post Graduate Studies Center in Imphal, Manipur. From 1980-1982 he was assistant editor of the highly respected Hindi literary magazine *Purvagrah*, and he served in other cultural capacities in Bhopal. Since 1982 he has lived in Delhi.

Within a year or two of his first arrival in Delhi, he began writing poetry and short stories in Hindi. His first poetry collection was published in 1980, and his first collection of short stories was published in 1982.

In addition to writing poetry and literary prose, Uday Prakash is a translator, freelance journalist, director and writer for film and television. Through Rajendra Yadav, I first met Uday Prakash in 1988 in the offices of *Dinman,* then a major Hindi weekly newsmagazine. We have corresponded ever since, and I made trips to India in 1991 and 1995 to visit with him and other Hindi authors, particularly Mudra Rakshasa.

Uday Prakash is a voracious reader. He has read the complete works of the major writers and poets of Hindi literature, and he has read most of the major work of all other Hindi writers past and present. His own writing, therefore, is firmly based in the history of the Hindi language(s) and its (their) literature(s). In addition to that, however, he has been profoundly influenced by other authors whom he has read in English translation. Prominent among those are Bruno Schulz, Jorge Luis Borges, and Mikhail Bulgakov (especially *The Master and Margarita*). More recently he has been excited by the work of Isaac Bashevis Singer and of Milorad Pavic, especially the latter's *Landscape Painted With Tea.*

I have read all of Uday Prakash's work, and I have so far translated a half dozen of his poems and nineteen of his stories. Because of the publisher's restriction on the number of pages, we present here only thirteen of his stories. One story we have not included, "Duty Officer: Duddoo Tiwari, "is available at http://www.paperplates.org/

pbytes.html, one of the "paperbytes" of the Canadian online literary magazine *paperplates.*

The first story of Uday Prakashs I read, and translated in 1988, was "Tirich." Its initial humour and its later straightforwardly-expressed and powerful pathos made it clear I had found a talented, troubled, serious and humorous author. Since then, Uday Prakash has become even more troubled by the world around him, particularly the political, social and cultural climate of Delhi, which he sees as becoming increasingly harsh, inhumane and immoral, especially in its higher strata. Yet he has not lost his humour or sense of romance. The story, "Delhi's Wall" (*Hans*, December, 2001), though a powerful indictment against casteism and official oppression of the poor, is a love story. While Uday Prakash seems to pick up his pen (or now, boot up his computer) primarily out of rage, the ink he uses seems infused with revelry and romance. In this way Uday Prakash is similar to Bertolt Brecht. While motivated by an urgent need to use literature to make the world a better place, the didactic element of Uday Prakash's stories is subservient to the tale itself. May it ever remain so, because then it is more powerful. If it were to take the main focus, the story would be ruined and the "point" would become lost in the spotlight or seem trite and trivial.

The overriding principle by which we have arranged these stories is this: stories set in a village or small town precede those set in Delhi or a large city. This reflects generally the life of their author, whose two major places of residence have been rural Chhattisgarh and urban Delhi, in that chronological ordcr. If the reader would prefer to read these stories chronologically, then here they are, in chronological order by year of first publication in Hindi:

Tepchoo 1982, *Tirich* 1988, *Heeralal's Ghost* 1989, *Nailcutter* 1989, *The Golden Waistchain* 1989, *One Eay in the Life of the Indian Ivan Denisovich* 1989, *The Correct Answer* 1994, *The Helper* 1994, *The Third Degree* 1994, *Job Search* 1994, *The Professor's Moan* 1994, *The Wall* 1994, *The Professor's Quilt* 1997.

I have met a number of people, in many walks of life, whom I felt I could have easily become if I had been born in a different time or place or if I had turned right rather than left at one or more junctures in my life. The "accident" of the time and place of one's birth determines to a large extent how one is raised, the language one speaks, and the attitudes, assumptions and predispositions one "inherits" from the society. Uday Prakash and I are two very different people, but if I had been born in January of 1951 in Chhattisgarh rather than in March of 1951 in Los Angeles, California, then I hope I could have become him or someone fairly close to him in personality and ability.

Of course, I am not Uday Prakash, and Uday Prakash is not Robert A. Hueckstedt. These English translations are not the same, and they certainly do not replace, the Hindi originals. Nevertheless, he and I have worked closely together on them. I have never guessed. I have asked not only about the meanings of words and phrases of which I was doubtful, but I have also asked about motivations and about intended suggestions. It has been an exhilarating and inspiring experience for both of us, and we are proud to offer these translations to readers of English.

Many argue, and rightfully so, that poetry, or great literature in general, cannot be translated. And that is exactly why we translators try to translate it. Jorge Luis Borges wrote that only that which is great in poetry is what gets translated. The rest can be changed or not translated at all and it would not diminish the greatness of the translation. To his mind, the translation was a further refinement and perhaps even, therefore, a greater work than the original, just as, in his opinion, the act of reading is superior to the act of writing.

We wouldn't want to go that far ourselves, but given our experience producing these translations, we would like to offer a classical Indian analogy for how we conceive of them. In his *Dhvanyaloka* (1.4), Anandavardhana compares a poem to a beautiful woman. The rasa of the poem is like the woman's soul.

The words of the poem are like her bones, muscles, etc. The *alankara-s,* the poetic ornaments of the poem (simile, metaphor, alliteration, etc.) are like her bracelets, necklaces, earrings, etc. These translations have the rasa of Uday Prakash's originals, or something close to it. That rasa is evoked by English words that necessarily have a different sound and form from the Hindi words, but they constitute a beautiful woman nevertheless. And that woman wears ornaments similar to those worn by her elder Hindi sister, without whom she would not exist.

While being proud of the work presented to the reader here, I am also humbled and well aware of the impossibility of the task I have attempted. If the reader enjoys these stories, I guarantee that the reader will enjoy the Hindi originals just as much, if not more. I thank Uday Prakash, my much respected elder brother, for being his wonderfully creative self and for his patience with my questions. I also thank my colleagues at the University of Virginia, Griff Chaussée and Chris Merrill, who read and helped to improve these translations.

Robert A. Hueckstedt
University of Virginia
Charlottesville, Virginia, USA

Heeralal's Ghost

The story of Heeralal is told in every home in the village of Rampur. When night falls, when the hearths grow cold, when the few bronze and brass pots have been washed and set in the corner, and when people get under their rags, blankets and sackcloth and fight against the cold with their own warm breath, they often talk about Heeralal.

Heeralal was born in this very village. People say that the day he was born, the earth shook and Ramji Patel's dandy nephew died of a snakebite. All night an owl hooted from the walls. A mysterious, haunted and frightening night that was. Just eight hours after giving birth to Heeralal, his mother died from hemorrhaging. In the village lay two corpses, and Heeralal shrieked for joy. Bela's mother says: "Heerawa didn't cry at all. Not one drop rolled out of his eyes. He just shrieked and hurled his tiny fists in the air. The most ominous thing, though, was that he was born with all his teeth, and his head was covered with thick, curly black hair. Beside him lay the body of his mother, his father Sudhanna was beating his forehead against the side of his cot, and Heerawa just shrieked and laughed."

Bela's mother felt sorry for him. In what unfortunate and difficult circumstances was Heerawa born! No sooner born than motherless. But his mother had to die. What was left of her, after all! Flakes of blood came out when she coughed. Rheumatism had stiffened her joints. How long could she drag on! With his birth Heerawa had saved her. Now he'll suffer. Sometimes he'll get rice water to drink, sometimes a couple ounces of goat's milk. Bela's mother's heart went out to him. She picked Heeralal up and put him in her lap, at which point he immediately stopped his shrieking and fixed his deep eyes on her. He had not yet been cleaned off. His whole body was smeared with blood and mucus. Not long ago he was in the womb of a living woman. Now she was dead.

Bela's mother felt Heeralal's eyes pierce deeply inside and enter her heart. There was nothing at all infantile about the way he looked at her. She felt his eyes burn inside her like a lamp, exposing all her sins. She became afraid. She broke out in a sweat. Never again did she put Heeralal in her lap.

Heeralal's entire childhood was spent in dirt and dust. By the age of five he had to herd the goats and gather wood from the jungle. Sometimes his father Sudhanna drank country liquor at Thakur's house, came home drunk and demanded his dinner. By the age of seven Heeralal had learned how to cook. Sudhanna's arms and legs were as thin as broomsticks, but his belly was a bottomless pit. He ate like a demon. If there wasn't enough food, he'd take it out on Heeralal.

People never noticed that Heeralal had stopped speaking. He was never seen playing with children of his age. He just worked, continuously. He gained such a deep and minute understanding of the nature and illnesses of goats that he was always called whenever a goat in the village fell sick. He would feel it, look at it intently and then go and bring back some leaves from the jungle. But he didn't speak. He didn't laugh either. There's only one incident in which people say he laughed.

What happened is this. Malkhan Chaudhari, one of the village's important farmers, had two sick buffaloes. Both were good milkers. Malkhan had a lot of good property. He had a tractor. For irrigation he had a diesel pump. He had eight bonded labourers, who worked day and night. Whenever some poor villager had to sell his land, the buyer was always Malkhan. His buffaloes had fallen sick, so Heeralal was summoned. He looked at them and felt them. He passed his hands over their necks and haunches, then went away. At four o'clock in the evening he fed them each two tiny leaves. By morning both buffaloes had swelled up like elephants. Their dead bodies were four times larger than normal. That morning, when the village cobbler

Dhanuklal told Heeralal that the buffaloes had died and he had been summoned to skin them, Dhanuklal said that Heeralal laughed. A huge laugh. Thigh-slapping. Out of control. Dhanuklal told everyone about this only much later because he was afraid that if he had mentioned it that day, Malkhan would have had Heeralal arrested on suspicion. Dhanuklal felt a lot of pity for Heeralal, who was motherless and silent. So he had kept quiet.

And, Heeralal kept quiet. People say that sometimes, while grazing the goats in the jungle, he'd sing. But his songs never had any meaning. One song, for example, was: O mother-in-law of my son, what a mixed up mess in your skirt.

Heeralal was seventeen or eighteen years old when he started working regularly in Thakur Harpal Singh's haveli. That same year he was married to Phuliya, a fashionable daughter of Phoolchand Gwaale, of the village of Pondi. The Rampurians said she'd never stay with a mute, inept fellow like Heerawa, she'd have affairs all over the place, and before long she'd pack up her pots and pans and disappear. But, that's not how it happened at all. She stayed right where she was, with Heerawa. Also that same year Sudhanna fell ill. For four days, despite his sickness, he continued working, weeding the fields of Harpal Singh. From early in the morning on the fifth day he had a very high fever. When Thakur's overseer Lalla Pundit came in the morning to call him for work, Sudhanna lay in the courtyard, his face covered with a towel. Lalla Pundit said, "So, you lazy son of a bitch, you're going to pretend to have tuberculosis so that you can have a good time at home and flirt with your young daughter-in-law?" Sudhanna didn't move a hair. Lalla Pandit swore at him and poked him with his stick, but Sudhanna just lay there like a wooden board. Covering her face, Heerawa's bride came and said, "Leave him alone, Panditji, he's got a very high fever." So Lalla Pandit said, "So who's going to weed Thakur's field, you little ... ! You go to his place then. Yesterday, when he begged a couple pounds of grain of us, he didn't think, today his arms and legs wouldn't work!"

Heeralal's wife Phuliya got ready and went to do the weeding in Thakur's fields in place of her father-in-law, and Sudhanna lay just as he was, his face in a towel, in the sunlight in the yard. In the afternoon, after grazing the goats, Heeralal returned, and as he strode intently through the yard to get some bread, he stumbled over Sudhanna and fell flat out. He saw that his father was dead. That same night Sudhanna was cremated. According to village tradition, except the households of important people like Thakur Harpal Singh, Lalla Pandit and Malkhan Chaudhari, in no homes that night was the hearth lit.

Heeralal did no mourning or crying. He remained silent as always. No one had ever seen him talk with Phuliya either. No laughter or banter, no arguments, no fights. Some people believed Heeralal had a weak mind and was a simpleton. Others said he understood everything and just kept it all to himself.

It fell to Heeralal to do everything in Harpal Singh's house: cut the wood, sweep the floors, plaster and whitewash the walls, pull enough water from the well for baths for about twenty, cut the vegetables, make the beds, fodder the cattle, make the dung cakes, wash the clothes, do the dishes, every night from ten to eleven-thirty massage Thakur Harpal Singh with garlic mustard oil, wash the night's dishes, bring goods from the bazaar, and then the little stuff-serve water, light the hookas, supervise the children's defecations, run and summon people, etc etc.

But Heeralal only listened, he never spoke. Sometimes at night he'd have a half-hour or so of free time, so he'd go to Sarala Baby's room, sit like a dumb block in front of the transistor and listen to the songs. It was difficult to guess what, after all, he was thinking. And as it was, he didn't have any time to think. From early morning he whirled through the entire haveli like a spindle. In the outer sitting room serving paan, tobacco and tea stood Heeralal; pulling buckets of water from the well and carrying them in by means of a bamboo yoke across his back was Heeralal; sitting in the courtyard and cutting vegetables was Heeralal; putting Vimala Malkin's little precious on his shoulders and running around with him was Heeralal. At the same time he could be everywhere. Sarala Baby would be knitting a sweater and she'd say softly, "Heeralal, water", and in no time Heeralal would be standing there with a glass or *lota* of water for her. The little precious would whine, "Peepee!" and Heeralal would be there to pick him up. In the sitting room Thakur Harpal Singh would open his paan box and say, "No cloves", and Heeralal would be there with cloves. Wherever, he would be there. His breathing echoed throughout the haveli. Everywhere one could hear the sound of his footsteps. In every dark corner his eyes shone like those of a cat in the wild.

It's impossible that Heeralal, omnipresent as he was, could not have witnessed the incident. This is what happened. About twenty-five yards from Thakur Saheb's haveli a guest house had been built, consisting of four rooms and a verandah. Guests and relatives who came from far away would stay there. The Record Keeper for the area, the Patwari, lived in the outermost room of that guest house. His name was Kulbhooshan Tiwari. He had done the records of the village for the past twelve years, and he would say, "When the month of Bhadon comes around, I'm going to become the District Record Keeper." He was thirty-five, thirty-six years of age. The hair at his temples had begun to go gray. His hairline was in retreat. His teeth had been stained by lime and catechu. He was always chewing tobacco, and at night he drank with Thakur Saheb in the sitting room. The people in the surrounding villages were afraid of him. His area was fairly extensive. It had twenty villages in it. He took bribes. Making the rounds of the sub-district offices and the courts, the people were harassed, but whatever Tiwari wrote down was treated as God's Word. Heeralal's father Sudhanna had owned an acre and a half of land, but three years ago, right after Sudhanna's death, Kulbhooshan Tiwari had signed over the ownership of that land to Harpal Singh, and Thakur Harpal Singh had said to Heeralal that his father Sudhanna had sold him that land before he died. So Heeralal had absolutely nothing left. Even his thatched hut, from a legal point of view, now stood on Harpal Singh's land.

So this is what happened. That day, in the evening, Heeralal had gone off tc the bazaar to get some things for Thakur Saheb's house. Since the afternoon dishes had been left unclean, Phuliya had gone there to wash them and finish up some other work. It must have been seven o'clock that evening when Thakur Saheb called Phuliya, gave her some paper and the accounting ledger and told her to go give them to Tiwari Saheb.

As soon as Phuliya reached his room, Tiwari Saheb grabbed her, chained the door from inside, and turned the volume on the radio up as loud as it would go. The last thing that was Heeralal's, his wife's honour, was then taken away. A half-hour later Thakur Harpal Singh, too, came in the room, and on Tiwari Saheb's bed Phuliya's cries grew even louder. Later, they each gave Phuliya five rupees.

Heeralal got what he had been sent for and came back. He was quiet, as usual. He was tired. That night he gave Thakur Saheb his hour-and-a-half massage and returned home to find Phuliya awake and crying. Heeralal spread out his bedding himself and went to sleep. At two o'clock he got up. Phuliya was still crying. Heeralal put a hand on her head and said, "Don't fret. Sleep quietly. With the ten rupees I'll buy you a sheet to ward off the cold." Phuliya stared at him, her eyes wide open. How did he know about the ten rupees and that whole incident? But Heeralal's voice had the effect of a cooling ointment that extinguished all her grief and anger with a hiss. Her wet eyelids slowly dried, and she sank into a deep sleep.

Phuliya was consoled by the fact that not only could this stone of a man speak, but he understood, too. After that night, every other night or so Phuliya had to sleep with the Patwari. Sometimes Heeralal would even be working in the haveli, splitting wood or foddering the buffaloes, while Phuliya was over in the Patwari's room. Heeralal would come home after midnight and go to sleep. He had mastered such a silence that trying to understand what was going on inside him was not only impossible for Phuliya, it numbed the brains of everyone. Every villager knew, though, that Heeralal had been stripped of everything, from his own land, property, life and sweat to the honour of his woman. Heeralal's cheeks were sunken, the bones of his neck stuck out, his hair was dishevelled and matted with dust and sweat, from lack of sleep his eyes were red and dull and seemed on the verge of bleeding.

Heeralal took on even more work. He didn't leave even one moment for himself. If he was caught up with work, he'd sweep the entire haveli again, split more wood, or draw more water from the well and saturate the back garden. Sarala Baby, Vimala Malkin, Mrs. Thakur, the old grandmother, everybody sang his praises. Phuliya, though, had her heart in her mouth. Heeralal had turned into an uneasy jinn.

One night Phuliya's eyes opened at two or two-thirty. She saw Heeralal squatting and very forcefully moving his lower jaw up and down. First, Phuliya thought he was probably eating something, but then she saw his mouth was empty. Because of the power he was putting into his chewing, Heeralal's face was drawn tight, he rolled his eyes up and exhaled forcefully, with a hissing sound, and then he started chewing that invisible thing again. Occasionally, she could hear the clattering of his teeth.

Phuliya was scared. It looked like Heeralal had lost his mind. Suppose he went totally crazy and strangled Phuliya or cut her up with the short-handled axe. How could he be trusted? Frightened, Phuliya stopped breathing. Then she heard come out of Heeralal's throat a frightening, terrifying roar. Was he turning into a jinn before her very eyes? Phuliya was terrified. But it wasn't a roar. Heeralal was crying. His whole body contracted, then swelled, and his suppressed tears burst out in fits and starts. It was a pitiful, heart-rending cry that involved not just his face but his whole body, his lungs and his soul.

Phuliya got up. Her entire body was melting with sorrow. She placed a hand on Heeralal's forehead. He was startled. He became again just as he had been. Quiet and calm. He stood up, went outside to urinate and then went to sleep.

Heeralal increased his work hours even more. Now he gave the Patwari's room a full cleaning, too. He brought him tobacco and paan. Till eleven o'clock at night he massaged Thakur Harpal Singh, then he'd take his little bottle of oil over to Patwari Kulbhooshan Tiwari and give him a rubdown. Phuliya would have left not long before. The smell of Phuliya's sweat was still on Tiwari's body. Heeralal rubbed down and polished that same body with garlic mustard oil. He released every knot in the Patwari's muscles and relieved him of his exhaustion. Heeralal's face pulled taut, the veins at his temples swelled and snapped, he chewed on something invisible, but all the while he kept on massaging.

Now, he hardly slept two hours a night. Maybe not even that much. Because another time, at night, when Phuliya's eyes opened, Heeralal wasn't on his bedding. Phuliya got up and looked outside. There in the yard, in the terribly cold winter months of Poos and Magh, Heeralal was standing as still as a tree, totally naked, his entire body covered by a white layer of frost. Phuliya screamed. Her scream startled him, and he came back in like a statue of stone, his face completely emotionless.

Guests came to Thakur Saheb's house. It was the first anniversary of his father's death. The haveli was stuffed with forty to fifty more people. They were staying for ten days. Heeralal became a machine. Work work work. Water water water. Dishes dishes dishes. Wood wood wood. Heeralal would appear everywhere and then disappear. He manifested things right out of the air. The husband of the sister of the wife of the Thakur Saheb from Allahabad would say, "O Heerawa! A glass of water!" and Heeralal would have it for him. The wife of the middle one of the Thakur Saheb brothers would say, "Heerawa! Fuel's out!" and before she could blink her eyes, the yard would be filled with about ten maunds of wood. Seventy people had to bathe, the clothes of seventy people had to be washed, feasts for seventy, the dishes of seventy had to be cleaned. By the fourth or fifth day the guests were saying that Heeralal was doing all his work while sleeping. At night Sarala Baby had seen him come to the large water pot, fill a *lota* with water, give water to the guests and go away, all with his eyes closed. She was sure he was sleeping because he was snoring. To find out, the wife of the middle Thakur Saheb hid behind a door leaf. Heeralal was returning from the sitting room with a serving tray of paan. There Thakur Saheb, the Police Superintendent, Patwari and some other men were playing parcheesi. When Heeralal came through the doorway, Thakurain splashed water in his face. Heeralal woke up, and the serving tray slipped from his hand and fell.

Heeralal was reduced to a walking skeleton. He was only twenty-six years old, but looked as if he had been living for centuries. Among the guests were some snobby, spoiled "princes". What happened to Phuliya during their stay the whole village knew. Phuliya stopped having her period and was starting to show.

When Phuliya was in her seventh month, Heeralal had massaged Thakur Saheb and the Patwari and was on his way home at one o'clock in the morning when a mad dog came running through the darkness out of nowhere and sunk his teeth into Heeralal's ankle. Heeralal screamed. His cry passed through the village all the way to his house, and Phuliya was stricken with terror. She loved Heeralal more than her own life. Those days she was unable to walk, and the Patwari was forced to spend his nights alone.

A little while later Heeralal arrived groaning. His right leg, from the knee down, was covered with blood. The dog hadn't bitten just once but many times. Those days Phuliya was unable to cook, so Heeralal brought food home from the Thakur's. That food had occupied both his hands, so he had used his legs to try to kick the dog away. The dog had bitten him as many times as he had kicked it. Heeralal washed his legs with water, went outside, applied mud to his wounds, ate and went to sleep.

Seven days later Heeralal's body started swelling–his face, arms and legs. He started getting the shakes, and foam came out of his mouth. That was the first day that Heeralal didn't go to work at Thakur's haveli. No one from there came to see how he was, but Bela's mother, who had since become old, brought a message from the haveli to the effect that Sarala Baby and the middle wali Thakurain felt he shouldn't shilly-shally but go right away to the city and get a rabies shot. Otherwise, it would be difficult to survive the bite of a mad dog. Heeralal remained silent. Bela's mother brought some food from her own home. That day Phuliya was very sick, too. She was unable to move around, and her feet had swollen up like two balloons. Bela's mother cursed the Thakurs. As long as Heeralal had a breath left in him, he worked in their haveli like a whole phalanx of jinns, but now that he was sick, not one of them could come and see him. And that wretched Patwari didn't even have the decency to see how the woman was getting along who was carrying his baby.

These big, important families would lose some of their dignity if they came to see Heeralal. Acting wickedly, though, doesn't seem to have any such effect.

That night Heeralal suffered from a very high fever. His whole body trembled like dry grass in a hot wind, his eyes bulged out, and the foam kept rising out of his mouth. Somehow, Phuliya got up, picked some tulsi leaves, extracted the juice from them and gave it to him to drink, but it had no real effect.

It was after midnight, probably around one-thirty. The watchman had rung twice. A number of times. Phuliya had already been carried away into the cyclone of sleep. Then she heard the sound gon-gon. It was a heart-rending, terrifying sound of unfathomable pain, from deep within some machine. It couldn't be from any human. No man's throat could produce such a sound. It rose out of her hut and radiated through the darkness over the entire village. Those who heard it were stricken by fear and latched their doors. An owl began hooting. The jackals in the jungle started crying. Heeralal's body lay absolutely still, and the sound kept coming from his throat.

Heeralal was barking. Like a mad dog. But it wasn't just a bark. It was a heart-rending sound midway between barking and weeping. Phuliya began crying in torrents. She herself had a high fever. The pitiful sounds of a beast and a woman reverberated that night throughout the entire village. The Patwari, Thakur Saheb, Malkhan Chaudhari, Punditji, the middle wali Thakurain, all of them heard it, and covered their heads with their quilts. Dhanuklal, Paramesvara, Sambharoo, Kodoo, Ramcharan, Duasiya, Bela, everyone's eyes welled up with tears. No one could sleep. Fear and pity immobilized the entire village, petrified in the night's darkness.

The next morning, with much difficulty, in spite of his stiff tongue and the foam that kept secreting in his mouth, Heeralal was able to communicate that he needed to eat stuffed chillies and mango pickle from Thakur's house. Bela's mother went to the haveli. Weeping, she explained to Sarala Baby and the middle wali Thakurain, "The taste buds of a dying man become sharper. Before dying, a man gets unusual cravings. It looks like Heerawa won't survive."

The middle wali Thakurain was slicing suparees. She said, "Heeralal's paying for his sin. I heard that he poisoned Malkhanji's buffaloes."

Bela's mother was stunned. It wasn't enough that they sucked out of Heerawa all his blood, sweat, land, property, work and his wife's honour, but this haveli didn't even have a straw's worth of pity for him! She wanted to shout out, "Sin isn't going to drown Heerawa, it's going to drown you, you cannibals. There won't even be a place for you in hell! Without moving your big fat bellies, you all sit around enjoying yourselves, all at the expense of Heeralal's life! Fleas'll infect the Patwari and Thakur Harpal! They'll break out in leprosy! Instead of turds you'll all shit pus! Just have a look at the hell hole of your own sins! You send a message to Heeralal to go get an injection in the city, but did you offer to pay for the shot or the medicine? And that asshole Patwari ... Lord knows what poisonous germ he put in Phuliya's belly that's made her whole body turn blue, given her a fever and made her face swell up like a pumpkin ... !" But, Bela's mother held her tongue. She got one stuffed chilly and one piece of pickled mango in a sarai leaf and returned to Heeralal's. When the Thakurain had given Bela's mother the pickle for the dying Heeralal, she didn't even open her hand. She just flung it. As if he were a dog.

A dog, in fact, Heeralal had become. When he was given the pickle, he sniffed it, licked it a little with his tongue, and then left it. His tongue hung out like that of a panting dog, all nine inches of it. Human beings don't have tongues that long. All day a crowd of villagers hung around his house. A line of them passed through to look at him. The cobbler Dhanuklal performed an exorcism. Manraakhan Bhagat came from the village of Pondi, worked magic on a ball of flour and pulled some of the dog's hair out of it. Sudhanna's best friend, Old Man Tilkiya, burned some benzoin and castor oil leaves and chanted oyer Heerawa. Phuliya continued crying and writhing in her own pain. The villagers didn't realize it, but her heart was breaking.

Seven o'clock that evening Heeralal put his palms together, acted as if he were touching someone's feet, and still emitting the sound gon-gon, he succeeded in communicating the idea that he wanted to see Thakur Harpal Singh. Then he made an obscene gesture, imitated a tomato with each hand and put them both on his chest. Barely able to keep herself from laughing, Bela's mother realized that was an indication he wanted to see Sarala Baby, too. Seventy-year-old Old Man Tilkiya went to the haveli to give them Heeralal's message. Thakur Harpal Singh prohibited Sarala Baby from going because it had always been their tradition that no girl of the Thakur Family had ever gone to anyone's house in the village. He himself simply didn't have the courage to go. Deep down inside he was afraid. Heeralal couldn't be such a simpleton as not to know what had happened to his land and to Phuliya. From the very beginning he had been quiet and secretive. Suppose he suddenly bit him! Eight days after being bitten by a mad dog the man himself is full of the mad dog's venom. If Heeralal bit, not even Brahma would survive, even with a rabies shot, or even with all the rabies shots in the world. But the opinion of the village was powerful. If he didn't go, their attitude would be that as long as Heerawa was alive, Thakur's haveli had sucked out his blood, did whatever it wanted with his wife, and stole all his land and property, but when he was dying, no one from the haveli even came to see him. Yet Thakur Saheb was afraid. The mind of a silent man is the most dangerous. Who knows what Heerawa might do just before he dies!

Thakur Saheb felt he had to honour Heeralal's last wish. As a precaution, he took a thick stick along and stuck a pistol in his waistband, so that if Heeralal suddenly jumped to bite him, he'd smash in his skull and shoot him. Even the law allows a man to do that much in self-defense. Besides, who would agree to be a witness?

Harpal Singh stood ten yards away from Heeralal's little cot. Ramcharan put his mouth up to Heeralal's ear and shouted, "Thakur Saheb has come!" Heeralal barked. Three times. Then he turned his neck and cried, like a dog. His eyes were burning red coals. His tongue hung out and moved in and out slightly as he panted. Saliva hung from it and occasionally dripped to the ground. Then with his hand he indicated the touching of Thakur's feet, and suddenly, rolling over, he fell down out of the cot. The crowd scattered. People fled. There was no telling who he might bite. Thakur Saheb lost hold of his stick, and he completely forgot the pistol at his waist. He ran. The waistband of his dhoti came loose. He was in such a rush that he knocked over many others.

All the same, Heeralal didn't bite anybody. Like a four-legged animal, he followed Thakur Harpal Singh, barking and howling along the way. The villagers saw Thakur Saheb ahead, running toward his haveli, and behind him, moving on both feet and both hands, was Heeralal. Now and then he would bark and then cry in a most heart-rending, pitiful sound.

Ahead was a pit used as a reservoir for rain water. Now the water was all gone, but it was always muddy. When the water was gone, Thakur Harpal Singh had leaves, manure, and other waste piled in it for composting. People said it was that compost that made his fields produce gold.

Thakur Harpal Singh's eyes twinkled. Heeralal was still following him. Thakur ran around the pit and stood on the other side. From there he called to Heeralal as one would call a dog. One more time Heeralal barked and howled in that pitiful voice, then he tumbled down into the pit.

The people shouted. Once or twice the gon-gon sound came out of the pit, then all was quiet. Heeralal had gotten stuck in the mud. He was suffocating. Mud and manure had filled his nose and mouth. No one had the courage to go down and pull him out. Finally, Old Man Tilkiya and Ramcharan went down into the pit, tied a rope around Heeralal and pulled him out. He looked like a clay marionette. He had already died. On the other side of the pit stood Thakur Saheb and the Patwari. From the roof of the haveli all the women of the Thakur Family had watched the entire incident. In her own home, on the ground next to Heeralal's empty cot, lay Phuliya, unconscious. Alone.

Heeralal died at seven-thirty in the evening, and at eleven o'clock Phuliya died. When Phuliya died, Bela's mother and most of the village women were with her. Before dying, Phuliya suffered incredible pain. No one told her that Heeralal had died. When she indicated Heerawa's empty cot, the women said, Thakur Saheb had had Heeralal sent to the hospital. Phuliya's entire body was blue and swollen. At quarter to eleven she started writhing. Bela's mother forced her to drink a concoction of herbs. It was a case of miscarriage; ten minutes later Phuliya began flailing her arms and legs around, and blood started coming out of her vagina. Bela's mother says Phuliya lost probably four bucketsful of blood. The whole place was flooded with it.

Eleven o'clock that night, when Heeralal's pyre was burning on the edge of the pond, the village dogs suddenly started howling. The sky became unseasonably overcast, and rain started to fall. The air resounded with the roar of a storm. Lightning flashed, and the jackals in the jungle could be heard. The haveli was still, silent. A ghostly shadow covered the entire village. Then the village women saw a black, shaggy, yellow-eyed dog emerge from Phuliya's womb and run toward the haveli.

I do not know if there is any truth in that, but it certainly is true that when Phuliya died, she did not give birth to any child. Her whole body, despite losing so much blood, was immensely swollen. That very night, at two or two-thirty in the morning, Phuliya was burned next to Heeralal's pyre. For the cremation rites of neither Heeralal nor Phuliya did anyone come from the haveli. Not even the Patwari. It wasn't part of the tradition of the Thakur Family.

The rest of this story is true. It can be heard in every home in Rampura. Any child can narrate it for you.

Two nights later, the night of the uthawani ceremony for the ashes of Heeralal and Phuliya, the haveli's guest house burned down. The Patwari was there at the time. Somehow, he managed to escape, but all his important official documents were destroyed. He cried, beating his head, knowing he would lose his post. Some people said they had seen a ball of fire whoosh up out of the pit where Heeralal had died and land on the thatch roof of the Patwari's room. Others say the Patwari had had a lot to drink that night and was smoking in bed when he fell asleep and his quilt was the first thing to catch fire. After the guest house burned down, the Patwari started living in the haveli itself, in the west room.

On the fourth night after Heeralal's death, at eleven o'clock, someone knocked on the door of Thakur Harpal Singh's room.

Harpal Singh got up. He asked, "Who is it? A voice said, "You might be wanting your massage, Sir..." Thakur Saheb forgot for a moment that Heeralal had died. As was his habit, he opened the door. There was only a cold wind, that rattled his bones, and in which someone seemed to be breathing. Goosebumps rose all over his body, and he fled, stammering.

At midnight that same night the Patwari, Kulbhooshan Tiwari, had a full bladder he had to relieve. He left his room, crossed the verandah and went down the seven steps to the ground. There he was relieving himself against the wall of the haveli when he heard the sound of someone coughing behind him. He turned around and saw someone sitting on the steps, covered with a bright white cloth. The Patwari asked, "Who are you?" "I'm Heeralal," said the sheet, and began to stand up. As it rose, it became like a white column reaching to the sky. The Patwari started shaking. He began to lose consciousness. He wanted to scream, but only a thin whistling sound came from his throat. He urinated all over himself and blacked out. At seven o'clock the next morning he was picked up and brought into his room, only to find it reeking from feces all over the floor. The Patwari had a bump on his forehead from falling down on the stairs the night before, and now he had a high fever. People couldn't understand what he was muttering. They said he had had a seizure.

Every night after that, as soon as it grew dark, a heavy shadow hung over the village. An owl would sit on the parapet of the haveli and hoot in a frightening voice. Dogs would suddenly begin howling, and behind Heeralal's house a jackal would come and call out. It sounded just like a human being, sort of like the sound Heeralal made when he herded the goats. The doors of the haveli would be locked from inside, and all night long its residents would tremble in fear, sure that some calamity was hanging over their heads. All night the whole haveli resounded with Heeralal's footsteps. He could be heard panting everywhere. Not only that, sometimes Harpal Singh would be defecating in the latrine, and someone would latch the door from the outside. He'd be stuck for a long time and have to holler for help.

One night there really was an outrage. Sarala Baby felt someone had gotten on top of her and fondled her breasts. She tried to get up, to speak, to scream, but it was all useless. No part of her body would cooperate. Then everything went still. It wasn't late yet. Suddenly someone turned on her transistor as loud as it would go, and in the morning, when she returned to her senses, she found herself without a stitch of clothing on, and there were unmistakable signs she had been raped.

Well-known and highly-respected exorcists were called in. Sacrifices and havans were held. Ganges water was sprinkled throughout the haveli. Magical chants were recited. Incense, benzoin and oil creosote were burned. A number of tantriks conned Thakur Saheb, trapped Heeralal's ghost in a bottle, took the money out of Thakur Saheb's pockets and the bottle out of the haveli, and nothing changed at all. At night, sometimes Thakurain would bump into Heeralal in the dark; sometimes middle wali Thakurain's saree would catch fire while she cooked. Evil-repelling black strings were tied to the arms of Thakur Saheb and the Patwari, but every night something happened.

Not just Sarala Baby, middle wali Thakurain and Vimala Malkin, too, found themselves raped and naked in the morning. Thakur Saheb would be served his food, and as soon as he sat down to eat, the sharp smell of shit would start wafting from the food. He'd vomit. The lentil dish would be full of blood. The eggplant would turn into dog meat. When he got up in the morning, he found bones in his bedding. Sarala Baby suffered epileptic fits and started acting insanely. Sometimes she'd go naked into the Patwari's room and start hugging him.

One day Thakurain opened a jar of pickles only to find it was full of mud and manure. The basket full of fine, delicious laddus contained instead little bricks.

One night Thakur Harpal Singh's eyes opened to see Heeralal, as he always had been, in the flesh, sitting on the stool opposite his bed, smiling. The container of garlic mustard oil was in his hand. He said, "A massage, sir," and advanced toward him. Thakur Saheb had already lost consciousness, muttering unintelligibly.

Dhanuklal and Ramcharan say that one night, around midnight, Lord knows what happened in the haveli, but Thakur Harpal Singh was standing in his yard firing away his double-barreled, twelve-gauge shotgun, and Kulbhooshan Tiwari was screaming like a madman and smashing his lathi against the ground. Both were hollering and screaming uncontrollably. At the same time the jackal behind Heeralal's house was howling.

It was bruited about in the surrounding villages that the zamindar family in the haveli had lost its grip on reality. No one went there anymore. Once Shyamlal, a water-carrier in one of the villages, was tricked into taking a land problem of his there, and as soon as Thakur Saheb saw him, he grabbed a cudgel and screamed,

"Heeralal's come!...run Thakurain!...Heerawa's come!!" Who knew when he might be out of his mind and shoot off his gun, so no one passed by the haveli, even by mistake.

Within six months the haveli was in ruins. Sarala Baby started to show, and the Patwari took her with him and escaped. People say she gathered up the family's entire treasure of gems and jewelry and took it all with her. And just what was the Patwari going to do with an epileptic? He was a piece of slime from the start. He probably got his hands on the treasure and sold Sarala Baby in Delhi or Bombay somewhere. Middle wali Thakurain went back to her parents and never returned. Thakur Harpal Singh became as thin as a thorn from all the emotional stress. He was afraid of everyone. His relatives convinced him to go on a pilgrimage with Thakurain and Vimala Malkin. That was seven years ago, and no one knows what happened. Some say they all became sadhoos and fakirs. Others say they were on a boat in the Ganges at Haridwar that flipped over, and they all drowned.

The haveli is still right where it was. Moss and grass have taken hold all over. No one has the courage to look through the cracks of the locked doors. What would be left in a haveli that had been empty for so long? The owl can still be heard there hooting at night. Many people say, they saw with their own eyes that Heeralal and Phuliya were living there. At night they both ate paan and spat all over the place. During the day many people have seen the marks of their red spit.

I can't say how much truth there is in this whole story. Perhaps the Thakur family were ruined by their own fear. Everything they saw was simply a manifestation of that fear. Some people say this whole affair was put on by the sons of the harijans, cobblers and landless labourers of the village. Full of hatred, anger and a desire for revenge after Heeralal's death, they were the ones who organized and orchestrated this whole play of ghosts and brought the haveli to ruin. Those young men had been to the city, had been educated a little, and were party members. Others say no, Heeralal actually became a ghost. He lives in the haveli even today. That's why people call it the Haunted Haveli.

All the same I have no idea what's true and what's false. Just a few days ago I went to the village of Rampur for a wedding. I saw the haveli. Pigeons and bats live in it. It's completely desolate and still. Anybody going there would be afraid. Its bricks have disintegrated. Here and there long grass has taken root. Moss covers everything.

The people of Rampur are all agreed, though, on this. No one knows who, but at night somebody must be watering the haveli's back garden. It's full of guava, orange and plum trees. The fruit they bear are deliciously sweet and big, and the boys from the village pick them and lick their lips and fingers in delight.

The Helper : A Memory Fragment

One of Father's characteristics was that he was always eager to help others. Even if people didn't really need his help, Father was still usually able to find some way to help them out.

If someone just happened to visit, Father was certain he must be in some sort of trouble; and if the visitor was too shy to open up and explain his problem, Father would verbally manoeuvre left, right, up, down and around in an effort to find out just what the trouble was and how he could provide assistance.

Many people simply didn't have that many problems, or they knew they were perfectly capable of solving them themselves. People like that made fun of Father.

Other people knew very well what Father's limits were. They knew how much help he could be in various circumstances, and they knew when he could provide no help at all. In other words, they knew Father's status, usefulness and abilities. When such people needed Father's help, they got it, and when they felt he wouldn't be able to be useful, they made sure not to tell him about their problem.

For example, Father did not have much acquaintance with state cabinet ministers, industrialists, smugglers and important bureaucrats, so he couldn't do much for the important people in the market town or the city. All the same, if they were to come to him and cry about their problems, Father would have always made some attempt to help them.

Nevertheless, there were many people who really did need Father's help, and for them he was useful. For example, in someone's home someone was sick and needed to be taken from the village to the hospital, and they had no money for medicine or the doctor. In a situation like that, Father could be helpful. He'd load the patient on his tractor, take him to the hospital in the market town, get him admitted and often spend his own money.

There was an aboriginal called Laloo who was suffering so much from TB that, although he was only twenty, he looked like he was eighty. He had withered away to just skin and bone, and every time he coughed, he spat up blood. After Father sold our grain, he took Laloo to Bhopal. Two years later, Laloo came back, cured. Now no one could look at him and say that two years ago he was just centimeters away from the jaws of death.

Laloo would always come to our house early in the morning. Usually, he would bring us green vegetables, tomatoes and the like. After he got well, he started growing vegetables, and that was how he expressed his gratitude to Father.

The incident I am about to tell also has to do with Father's habit of helping others.

It was the monsoon season. For a number of days the rain had fallen steadily. With occasional short breaks. All the ponds and ditches were overflowing. The jungle was drenched. The verandahs were full of water.

The river that flowed by our house was in spate. Through the middle of it flowed a current of eddying dirty water. Froth, broken trees, and flotsam and jetsam from God knows where were all bobbing up and down in the swift current.

The river had become frightening. The sight of it and the sound of its waves caused us to tremble. At night, or even during the day, if you were to stand near the frothing river and close your eyes, you would feel as if you were surrounded by the flood, as if you were in the middle of the current.

The bridge had not yet been built. A rowboat was used to cross the river. Into the riverbank a ghat had been built, a flight of stairs down into the water. The boatman charged an anna or two to take you across.

During the monsoon season our village was usually totally cut off from the market town and the city. But every Wednesday a bazaar was set up in the market town that was crucial for many of the villagers. They went there not merely to buy things but to sell their own things as well. So every Wednesday, from early in the morning, there was always a crowd of people waiting to cross the river, and all day that day the rowboat never got a rest.

The incident I am about to relate occurred on a Wednesday, bazaar day in the market town. Despite the flooding of the river, group after group of villagers kept arriving at the ghat to cross the river in order to go to the bazaar. Low in the water with the weight of the people and their wares, the boat would go out over the swift current, cross the river, let the passengers out and come back.

Clearly, the same number of people who crossed the river would want to recross it after the bazaar was over. The ferrymen's bags were filling up with coins that had on them the face of either George V or Queen Victoria.

Gradually, evening fell and darkness gathered. It was the dark fortnight, when the moon, when it did appear, provided little light. Here and there in the village small clay oil lamps and lanterns started to twinkle. Every place else was immersed in a solid black darkness that carried inside it the noise of the flooding and frothing river, the sounds of lightning bugs flying hither and thither, the sounds of the cattle and hens, and the calls of frogs, purple coots and crickets.

As soon as it got dark, Father would always get out the booze. Some other villagers would also sit and drink with him. They would talk about life and death, politics and fanning, etc.

That was a time when Hindi poets and writers were not unknown to people in the villages. Father had memorized a number of poems of Pant, Nirala and Maithilisharan Gupta. Often he would sing Bachchan's Madhushala while he drank or afterwards.

Father was sitting and drinking with three or four others when somebody came and said there had never been so many people coming back from the weekly bazaar. Even if the boat never stopped, it would still take four or five hours to get everyone across.

The problem was the opaque darkness. Even with a lantern on board, rowing the boat was dangerous because the lantern provided only a small circle of light and made everything else that much darker. On their part, the boatmen were afraid of rowing, while the villagers on the other side of the river were anxious to get home. They had all left their homes just as they were, expecting to be back the same day, so getting back home was absolutely necessary.

It was very dangerous to row the boat in such darkness, through such a flood and with so many people. As it approached the ghat in the darkness, it could smash against debris or the trunk of a tree and overturn.

If some way could be devised to provide a little light, then everything would be easy.

By then, Father had already drunk quite a lot, and liquor only intensified his natural inclination to help others.

And he had an idea how to help. He started up his tractor, shifted its headlamps up a little and headed out toward the riverbank.

He stopped the tractor on the slope of land that was above the steps that led down into the river. When he put down the accelerator, the light from the headlamps became brighter, providing just enough light so the boatmen could see their way.

The boat then set out, carrying people from that side to this. After drinking, many times Father would ask, "Do you know the difference between virtue and sin?" Then he himself would recite in Sanskrit, "paropakaraya punyaya papaya parapeedanam" (Helping others is virtue, harming others is sin).

It must have been around midnight when the sound of people, at the ghat screaming and yelling could be heard. It was like a lamentation. Perhaps the boat had overturned.

I was young then. About ten years old.

In a little while the sounds of crying came from our house, too. Mother could be heard above all the others. She was going crazy. Sister-in-law, Auntie and the village women were crying, too. Carrying lanterns, everyone was heading in the direction of the ghat. I, too, was walking in that direction, along with my weeping mother.

About two-thirds of the ghat's steps were under water. The furious roar of the river was all-pervasive. People were screaming and shouting. Lanterns were scurrying here and there.

Then I realized the tractor wasn't sitting above the ghat. There was no light from its headlamps. There was just darkness and the flooding river. So Father...?

What a horrible experience. I felt as if a huge empty space had suddenly filled my heart. It was like a balloon that had been blown up, but it was empty, it had no air in it. My whole body trembled and I started crying.

I saw mother's bewildered face. She was writhing on the ground that was wet from the rain.

Perhaps what happened is while the tractor was on the slope of land above the ghat, either the brake slipped open, or the tractor somehow suddenly went into neutral, Father was in the driver's seat. The two or three men who were sitting on the pieces of wood that had been placed in front of the wheels jumped up and got out of the way, and the tractor headed down into the roaring river, taking Father along with it.

Somebody said that when that happened, Father was sitting down, drunk, and singing.

I know what he would have been singing, this poem by Tagore:

Jodi tor dak sune keuna asi, tobi ekala cholo re
ekala cholo, ekala cholo, ekala cholo re
(If no one responds to your call,
If no one listens to you,
Walk alone, walk alone, walk alone.)

Fortunately, not too far from the ghat was a sandbar, where the tractor's wheels became stuck. The tractor sank and the engine stopped. The water probably flooded its silencer.

I looked out in the feeble light of the lantern. Out quite a bit from the ghat, in the brown current of the frothing, rising river Father's head could be seen. I could only see the back of it. The tractor had sunk. On its seat, Father, too, had gone underwater to the top of his neck.

He did not turn around to look back in our direction. Fear had probably paralyzed him. His ears were full of the terrifying sound of the river, and all his eyes could see was the frothing, uncrossable flood.

We were all helpless. Father was a very big, heavy man. How could he be brought back from there to the ghat? The boat just then was at the far shore. He'd still be drunk. His head didn't go under because the seat of the tractor was quite high. If he tried to get down, off the tractor, he'd drown. He didn't know how to swim.

What I saw that night has always stayed fresh in my memory like a troubling picture. A night in the dark fortnight, a rain that had fallen steadily for days, the swirling noise of the frothing, foaming river rising between its banks.

And far out, in the middle of it all, paralyzed with fear, Father's head. Absolutely still.

If the tractor had somehow gotten into gear and its engine hadn't stopped, it would have gone out farther into the river. Then not even Father's head would have been visible.

But perhaps that was the day I learned we can all only be the observers of each other's dire emergencies.

After all, that day Father's head was in the middle of the flooding river, but all the rest of us, on the ghat, with lanterns, could do nothing more than run back and forth. My mother, too, crazed and crying, was just an observer. She could barely breathe; but between her and my father's head was a vast flood of water.

Although my heart was filled by a huge empty balloon and I was undergoing the most horrible experience of my life, I, too, was no more than a spectator.

Maybe Father knew all that, and that was why he didn't turn around to look back but just kept looking forward, in the direction of death.

Then Manohar picked me up. Perhaps he had been told to take me away from there. I writhed and wriggled, but he held me tight and took me home. I was still crying. I kept envisioning Father's paralyzed head drowning in the rising river.

Much later, lanterns and the sound of people talking were heading toward our home.

Manohar said, "Stop crying now. Father's coming."

The Third Degree

I should make it clear right off that this story is not merely based on some actual facts: the whole thing took place outside this text. Some stories are like that. What takes place in most stories does so only by means of and in the body of the language of the text.

This story therefore, should affect you somewhat differently. If it does not, then that proves it was unable to subdue you to its will. The incident is still to be completed in the external world, outside its text.

Granted, the external world itself is a text, a text of matter. It, too, is just as independent and whole within itself as a story is independent and whole within itself. The material text is not dependent on the literary text. That is, it can be said that some text of the external or material world existed when no literary text existed.

But that reasoning should not cause you to believe that the literary text is dependent on the material text or that it is a part of the external world, in the form of a commentary on it in another medium. In fact, the literary text, too, is self- contained, independent of the material text and whole within itself.

That is, when this whole external, material world did not exist, there was still the possibility of the existence of some literary text. Whether or not there was one is a question of time and circumstances. If there were no literary text then, and if the literary text became available only after the existence of the material text, then there are a number of possible reasons for that. For example, one reason could be that while some literary text in fact did exist, there was no Writer for it. Or perhaps Language–that is, the medium which could make that text perceptible and understandable to any particular group of human beings–did not exist.

Actually, the problem is that you and I, in fact everybody, is able to understand a literary text only when it is in a state of association with a material text. Because we, too, in fact, are matter and we are unable even to sense that which is not matter. For example, the text of a story.

In any case, in the external world, events taking place within the material text must change into a readable state before they can be included in a story. That is, in order for those events to be included in the text of a story, they have to take place again within, and through the medium of, language. That process has certain conventions and rules. So whether one wants to or not, a number of compromises must be made; the foremost of which is a compromise with Language itself, which is always changing, and is therefore perishable. Then there are conventions concerning the customary text of a story, followed by contemporaneous theories and presuppositions regarding what is communicable and what is understandable.

The result is that, even unwillingly, the story's text is so fashioned that it cannot possibly do justice to the text of the material event, and the entire effort becomes reduced to scribbling down an evanescent short story.

Therefore, the story I am about to present is not at all characterized by any new variations in the traditional structure of a short story, the textual conventions of a narrative, or in the area of literary language.

This story will cause scholars of narrative discourse and accomplished writers of fiction to groan in despair, and those writers who have earned their living their entire lives by regarding with doubt and suspicion every work of their contemporaries, except their own, will find much in this story not only to fuel that doubt and suspicion but also to deny this ordinary event the dignity of being called a short story.

This exceedingly long introduction may appear to you to be an unnecessary and pseudo-intellectual essay on literary theory fabricated in order to save a weak and unsuccessful story. It could also be a mesh of words that sprang into existence from the fear, lack of self-confidence, or pride of a dubious and unwelcome writer.

Now suppose I continue this introduction even further (the scope for that becomes greater with every sentence), and without presenting the, as it were, promised story I end this short story just with this introduction, then what would you do? Such stories, which are only an introduction to some unknown story, have already been written. It's a kind of style.

You must be familiar, though, with the story-telling and folklore traditions of India in which a preliminary, introductory or explanatory story constitutes a part of the main story. So if you criticize me for this introduction, I'll accuse you of being under the influence of Western and who knows what foreign traditions and conventions. Despite the fact that you are living in this country, this society, and the mythical world of the Indian people, you read our stories with Western eyes. You're a raggedy writer in the third world who has become a slave to Europe and the whites.

One true thing about this story (and you have to believe it or you should stop reading now) is that the event it describes is no more a part of the text of the story as your hand is a part of the ball of dough.

You must agree that when you eat a roti, you don't eat your hand as well. Likewise, when you read a story, you do not at the same time consume some other form of reality.

We'll let the critics eat their hands.

This event took place outside the literary text. Its main character is a friend of mine who has no particular relationship with language. For him, language is simply a tool.

After the death of my friend's father, his elder brothers abandoned their old and ill mother to the grace of God. My friend, whose name is Suresh, took her in, supported her, and after his marriage to Rajshri, whenever his mother and his wife argued, he always took the side of his mother.

Suresh was often aware that his wife was right, but he still took his mother's side because he reasoned, somewhat illogically, that even if his mother were wrong, she was going to die along with her wrong-headed notions in four or five years anyway, while his wife Rajshri was going to remain with him for many years after that. She was seven years younger than him, so it was also quite possible that she would even outlive him. So whenever his mother and Rajshri got into an argument, like a philosopher, he would contemplate time, and in his meditations his sixty-five year old mother would appear creeping along with polio and diabetes, and no sooner would she leave the house than she'd disappear down an open manhole in the street.

On the other hand, Rajshri's oscillating, full hips were visible far into the distance. Oscillating. The perpetual motion of his life and passion. One of Creation's gats composed in teental.

Sometimes he wondered whether or not the backing he gave his mother was based, in fact, on love for her. It seemed to him that the root cause for it was Rajshri's voluptuousness. The beauty, vigor, grace and attraction of her body, seven years younger than his, engendered within him a sense of inferiority, jealousy and anger, which was what really lay behind the support he gave his mother and the opposition he gave his wife. That is, the basic reason for the love he showed his mother was the antagonism he felt for the fullness of Rajshri's hips.

His in-laws were upset with him. From a sociological perspective this family seemed to them to be one in which the mother-in-law's authority and energy held sway over the husband. The wife in such a family is often afflicted by the mother-in-law and ignored by the husband. Therefore, Suresh's in-laws were always in sympathy with Rajshri and angry at Suresh. They could relate a number of incidents in which Rajshri was put down despite being in the right.

Yet Suresh's mother was not only the mother of Suresh. She had two other sons, both older than him. The responsibility for her welfare, for the rest of her life and until the completion of her final rites, was to be shared equally among the three brothers. The two elder brothers, therefore, were of the opinion that they should set their mother up in her own home, and the three of them would pay equal thirds of the rent and her daily expenses.

Suresh, however, disagreed. If she lived alone, and if the level of her blood sugar were to get dangerously high, and if she started getting the cold sweats and fell unconscious, and if she needed an immediate injection of insulin, then who would give it to her? She was a long-time sufferer of diabetes, and every other week or so such an incident happened.

Suresh owned a truck which was financed through the bank. He drove it himself. After the monthly payment to the bank and the expenses for gas, oil, maintenance and repairs, Suresh brought home a monthly income of three to four thousand rupees. But there was no work during the three months of the rainy season, so if you average that in, his monthly income was only two and a half to three thousand rupees. Four hundred rupees a month went for rent. It was low because he had lived in the same place for about fifteen years. Every month Suresh spent about three hundred rupees on cigarettes, paan, liquor and the occasional luxury of a chicken dinner. The remaining money went toward household expenses and whatever his wife and mother needed.

Which is to say they lived close to the bone, and it showed on his wife–a principle of family life outside the realm of sociology. At the end of February, when Suresh's wife was near her time to give birth, his in-laws had her come back. They got her registered at the hospital in Raipur, and while looking out for her welfare in every way possible, they made all the arrangements necessary for her first delivery. Behind all that care and attention was not so much their love for Rajshri but their desire to show how inferior Suresh and his mother were.

I'm sure you can understand that there is a connection between the event I'm about to relate and Suresh, an individual outside the text of this story. Suresh drives a truck. So far no organized, definitive study has been done on the connections between trucks and language, so there is little room for excellence in the use of language to describe this event.

Nevertheless, as I have said before with regard to Suresh, since this event took place outside the text of this story, and since it took place without even any thought of a story, I see no hope at all of being able to change its nature and confine it within the structure of this story.

The fact of the matter is that incidents that happen to a truck driver, a vegetable seller, a man who delivers newspapers, or a farmer, that is, to any real person in the real world–take place without any concern at all for language. They take place without making any attempt to become stories. They take place in that way all around us, every day, every moment, and continually. Even if you were to know everything about them, what effect could they have on the nature and mood, the structure and the text of the contemporary Hindi short story?

Suresh was a childhood friend of mine. About twenty years ago I came down with typhoid. My mother and father had already died. At the age of thirteen I had become an orphan. My elder brother had taken possession of our house and property. Having no money, not only couldn't I buy medicine, but I also went without eating for five days. It was then that Suresh stole two rotis and a plate of alu-gobhi from home and brought them to me. Sick with typhoid and having starved for five days, I sat up and ate roti and alu-gobhi, and I cried. I can still remember the taste of that food, and I still remember crying.

Those days Suresh and I studied together in high secondary. His mother, whom he was now taking care of and for the sake of whom he was fighting with his wife, terrorized him then much more than the others. In her opinion, of her three sons he was the most incapable, irresponsible and useless.

Every mother in the end, however, is a woman; and since the status of women in our society is still a precarious one, and they are generally dependent on others, a mother's psychology, to some extent, resembles that of a woman's.

Suresh's mother, as one of this society's women, weak and dependent, had no hope at all of any benefit from him in the future, so in her eyes, compared to her other two sons, who were sensible and worldly-wise, the status of Suresh was the lowest.

After their weddings, when her two elder sons took some things from the house and went away to live separately with their wives, Suresh's mother saw the light. She cursed her fate, her two elder sons and their wives, and she grabbed hold of Suresh and kept him near her.

She was always afraid that Rajshri would take him away from her, so the older she got, the sharper her tongue became with her daughter-in-law. The fight in her was a worn-out one born of fear, despair and helplessness, but Rajshri's youth and the fullness and voluptuousness of her hips, buttocks and arms gave it vigor and strength.

Suresh knew that. Despite being a truck driver he fully understood what was going on, and for that reason, with sympathy and compassion, he always sided with his mother.

Last March Suresh told me the incident I am about to relate to you. I don't remember who the country's Prime Minister was then. There have been too many names in too short a time for me to be able to keep them all straight.

This incident took place in Madhya Pradesh, in the small town where Suresh lived.

Suresh's in-laws had brought his wife to Raipur for her delivery. Back in his house, Suresh was alone with his mother. Since he was going to become a father for the first time, he was experiencing many new feelings that he was totally incapable of expressing, having a closer relationship with trucks than with language.

On the fifteenth of February, at nine o'clock at night, the postman came and gave Suresh a telegram. It was urgent, and it said:

Come To Hospital Immediately Stop Alls Well Sudhindra Kukreti

Sudhindra Kukreti was Suresh's eldest brother-in-law. He was a sales tax official who, in just five years of service, had been able to buy three MIG (Middle Income Group) flats in Raipur and rent them out. He was able to get quite a lot more than the going rates for them because all his renters were bureaucrats in one or another department of the state government. Sudhindra Kukreti was also a short story writer. He wrote revolutionary and feminist stories, and he was said to be a writer in the tradition of Premchand.

That same night Suresh went to the station and got a reservation for him and his mother on a train that left at six o'clock the next morning. Before going to bed, his mother made pooris and potato curry for the journey. Suresh bound up his bedding and organized his two attachés. His mother wasn't at all pleased that her daughter-in-law had gone back to her parents' home for her delivery. Didn't this town have hospitals, too? Women from all over have their babies here. Why did she have to go off to Raipur, show herself off and cause people unnecessary trouble?

At three-thirty Suresh was woken up by his mother. He used the latrine and brushed his teeth, etc. and was ready by quarter after four. They had little to carry, one bedroll and two attaché cases. His mother picked up one of the attachés, and they decided to walk out like that to the main street, where they would get a rickshaw for the station.

Their things were outside on the steps and Suresh's mother was putting the padlock on the door when a rickshaw came clattering out of the haze. With a long and harsh ringing, it came to a stop next to the steps. The rickshaw wallah said, "Oho, Suresh bhaiya, it looks like you're getting ready to go somewhere. Where are you going?"

Suresh was shocked. The rickshaw wallah was the town's famous thief Fakira. Sure, he pulled a rickshaw, but everybody in that small town knew that the connection between theft and Fakira was the same as that between smoke and fire. Wherever there is smoke, there is fire. Wherever there's been a theft, you can be certain Fakira was involved.

But what could Suresh do now? Fakira's already seen the padlock on the door, and from the bedroll and the attachés, he already knows that Suresh and his mother will be out of town at least for a few days.

There was nothing else they could do but let Fakira take them to the station. When they arrived, they still had a half hour before the train would leave. Fakira gave them superb service. He himself carried all their things to the platform. He brought them cups of hot tea, from a stall outside the station, special, with ginger and cardamom. When talking to Suresh's mother, he always called her "Maji, Maji", and he complained to her fervently about his wife's laziness and stupidity. And he himself got their reservations confirmed. All of which is to say that he now had them trapped. He now knew full well that they were taking a thirteen-hour train ride to Raipur, and from the size of the bedroll and the large attaché, it was obvious they wouldn't be back for at least a week or two.

As soon as the train arrived at the platform, the crowd rushed in. Fakira himself pushed and shoved his way in, found their berths and loaded their things. Then he cursed and swore at the people who had taken Suresh's and his mother's seats and pushed them away. Fakira himself then supported Suresh's mother through the crowd and led her to her seat. If he hadn't been there, getting settled in the train would have been much more difficult.

Suresh's mother offered Fakira fifteen rupees, but with righteous indignation he said, "No, no, Ma ji, it would be sinful for me to take that much from you! I'm just doing my duty. And we're just like family, aren't we? Since when did I become a stranger?" And only after much insistence on her part did he accept ten rupees. Then he continued, "I don't cheat anyone. I live off the sweat of my brow. It's only right. Only if you sweat do you have any right to dal and roti." The train jerked forward, but only when it began to pick up speed, at the last possible moment, did Fakira jump off, back down onto the platform.

Suresh was beside himself with worry. His mother became quiet, looking absent-mindedly out the window at the buildings and trees passing by. Angry at her, Suresh said, "Don't you understand anything? Fakira was so attentive, wasn't he? And there you were blessing him without even thinking! 'May you be prosperous, live long and be healthy.' Don't you realize that we've left our home back there, and Fakira's there, too? Do you think he'll leave it alone, he'll write first before taking anything? When we get back, you'll have an empty house to sweep. Don't talk to me."

His mother too began to worry. Even though just a little while ago she had been calling Fakira "son" and blessing him, now she cursed him to the seventh generation. May that Fakira be damned and rot in hell! May leprosy break out all over the wretch! Who does he think he is bothering us from early in the morning!"

Suresh's mother said to him, "Leave me in Raipur and you get back here on the next train. Maybe, by the grace of God, nothing will have happened by then, and then we won't have to worry because you'll be here."

Suresh, too, had come to the same conclusion. His mother muttered and mumbled during the whole trip, remembering where each and everything was. Most of the old things her elder sons had taken away. All she had was what they had left behind. Suresh and his wife had purchased a color TV, VCR, and fridge, etc. on instalment plans. Then there was the little bit that their in-laws had sent. Yet, when she added it all up, she estimated that her house held property that would be valued at more than a hundred or a hundred and fifty thousand rupees.

As soon as he arrived in Raipur, Suresh learned that his wife had been in the delivery room for two days, and the doctors were now thinking of doing a Caesarean. He went to the hospital immediately, and outside the room he could hear the sounds of Rajshri's screaming and crying. He was astonished to see his mother suddenly turn compassionate. Her face all at once contracted with pain, and she began sobbing uncontrollably, in jerks. It was amazing that these two women, who had spent so much of their time and energy battling each other daily in an undeclared war, had now suddenly become so close to one another.

He could do nothing else now but remain in Raipur until his wife gave birth. If he were to abandon his wife in this condition, then his in-laws would feel even more justified in their charge that his wife was ignored and oppressed.

That evening Suresh went to the temple, and when he offered up his coconut to the god, Rajshri's screams reverberated in his ears; but in fact, instead of praying for the good health of his wife and soon-to-be-born child, his fervent prayer was that his home be safe from Fakira.

Three days later he was able to take the evening train back. At eleven-thirty that morning he had become a father. The hospital's nurses and cleaning staff and in-laws congratulated him, and he gave them all the customary gifts and tips. His mother saw to the welfare of both the child and the new mother, and Rajshri looked at her with gentle, grateful, content eyes.

A profound love for his wife arose in Suresh. For the past few months making love with her had been impossible. Now that she was out of the delivery room and in the maternity ward, her free, exhausted body filled him with urgent passion.

This entire episode had cost him 650 rupees, and that evening he caught the train for home. His writer brother-in-law, Sudhindra Kukreti, who was a sales tax official, and who was noted for writing in the tradition of Premchand, took him to the station in his Maruti.

At seven o'clock in the morning Suresh stood opposite his house. Right away he could see that Fakira had done his job. Another padlock, brass and unfamiliar, hung on the door latch.

In a little while Harpreet, the wife of his neighbor Amrik Singh, came out with a key and told him about the theft. Other neighbors, women and children came out and gathered around. Harpreet told him they were unable to send the news to him in Raipur because no one knew his address there.

Inside, the house had been cleaned out. Nothing was left–not the television, fridge, VCR, watch, radio, strong boxes or suitcases. Even in the kitchen, the pressure cooker and all the thalis, plates, bowls, ladles and spoons had been whisked away. Fakira had done his job in a precise and professional manner.

Suresh had put a lot of effort and energy into gathering all those things together, one by one. He started crying. It was as if he'd been raped. He dropped his attaché to the floor with a bang and went to the police station.

The SHO there was Ramkishore Pandey. He had been transferred here from Bakohi, and even when he was in charge there Suresh knew him, because Suresh had hauled coal from the nearby mine. Once, Pandey had taken a bribe from a contractor, and he used Suresh to deliver the stolen coal. From then on, the two of them were fast friends. Later, Pandey and Suresh teamed up to steal iron girders away from the construction site of a hospital.

When Pandey was transferred from Bakohi, it was Suresh who loaded up his family and all his belongings into his truck and brought them to the city.

As soon as SHO Pandey saw Suresh he said, "You're just the man we've been waiting for. Next time when you go away, give your address to the neighbors first."

Suresh told him all about their morning encounter with Fakira, and he summed up by saying, "I'm a hundred and one percent certain that Fakira's the one who did this."

Pandey replied, "Don't worry, yaar. We'll make Fakira give all your property back. We'll give him such a beating that not only will he give up burglaring for good, but he won't even be able to push a rickshaw anymore."

Suresh told him not to worry about expenses. The theft amounted to a hundred to a hundred fifty thousand rupees, maybe twice that. With emphatic authority, Pandey had the burglary report written up, and he suggested to Suresh, "Now you go home and take it easy. Within three days we'll make sure everything gets returned to you."

Suresh knew that if the police wanted to, they could get their hands on anything. His association with Pandey in Bakohi had taught him what the real connections were between burglars and the police, so he felt confident that by the time his mother and wife returned, everything would have been returned, and he could relate to them the whole story with delight.

Rajshri had given him a daughter. Now he knew what he was going to name her–Lakshmi the Goddess of Fortune. Before her birth Fakira had taken away their wealth, and after her birth, it had all come back.

Three days later, at about nine-thirty at night SHO Pandey arrived on his Rajdoot motorcycle. He was upset and said, "Things are all fouled up, yaar. It looks like we took the third degree too far. Fakira's dying. If he does die, I'm gonna lose my goddamn job. And some politicians are ready to turn this into a Hindu-Muslim thing."

Suresh, too, became upset and said, "So what can we do now?"

Pandey replied, "The problem is, this afternoon I got into a rage and filed papers for Fakira's arrest on another charge. I thought that once we got our hands on him and started beating him up, he'd spill the beans about burglarizing your house. That's why we can't let him go now without bail. I've already spoken with the SDM. He, too, is afraid of the possibility of Hindu-Muslim riots because of this. So

Fakira's bail has been approved. Everything's ready. All we need now is someone to sign for it."

Pandey went on to explain that no one was willing to do that because they were afraid either the bastard would die from his beating or he'd run away. Pandey said, "Suresh, yaar. My job's at stake here. You're going to have to post Fakira's bail. It was only because of your suspicion that we arrested Fakira in the first place. He even asked us. He said, 'Pandey ji, on what grounds are you arresting me?' I said, 'For urinating in a public place, you bastard. That's why.' For two days we hung him upside down and beat him, we thrashed him until you couldn't tell his outside from his insides, and we put his hands under a chair and jumped up and down on it, but the son of a bitch never confessed to burglarizing your house. Today at five o'clock Tripathi started jumping up and down on his chest, and that's when Fakira started throwing up blood. Now we've heard that Fakharu Mian is giving a speech over the mosque's loud speaker and turning this into a Hindu-Muslim thing."

Here a Supreme Court lawyer, who was himself a short story writer, expressed an objection. He said that the person whose house was robbed could not post bail for the alleged thief because he himself would have been the one to file the FIR (First Information Report). When Suresh related this incident to me, however, he had specifically mentioned that he himself had posted the bail.

We all know that judges, the police and criminals conduct their affairs outside the text of the Constitution. Here, too, differing recensions and variant readings exist.

But the esteemed lawyer who expressed this objection did not want to allow this incident to be used to breach or bring into contempt (if I can use that phrase) the text of the Indian Penal Code. Therefore, his considered opinion was that Fakira could be arrested for urinating in public, and on that charge the station's SHO would have the authority to accept bail and release the accused. Whether you agree or not, the required corrections have been made above.

Suresh went with Pandey to the station. The papers were drawn up. Fakira's condition was, in fact, serious. He had been beaten to a pulp. Blood had come out of his mouth and ears. It was impossible for him to walk.

Pandey loaded him into a Public Works Department jeep and took him to the hospital. Two days later he went there and found that Fakira was able to speak. He told Fakira that Suresh would pay for all his expenses. Whitewashing his own involvement in what had happened, Pandey reaffirmed his friendship for Fakira. Suresh was solely responsible for what had happened to him.

Fakira never complained to Suresh. All he said was, "Bhaiya, you really got me beaten up."

So far Suresh had spent thirteen hundred rupees on Fakira's food and medicine. He went to the hospital every day to bring him food and fruit. He said to him, "Look, Fakira. You know and I know that you were the one who robbed my house. There's absolutely no doubt at all about it. In the police station they almost beat you to death. Blood was coming out of everywhere. They even stuck a rod up your ass. A little more repair work on you like that and you would have been finished. Why didn't you ever confess?"

Peeling an orange, Fakira smiled and said, "First, Suresh bhaiya, I was a weakling. All it took was a couple of slaps for me to reveal where I'd sold the goods. I was scared to death of being beaten up. So I lost all respect at the fence, and the fencers refused to buy my stuff any longer. They all said I was a son of a bitch who could steal, but I didn't have any meat on my ass. Just a little scare and I'd shit in my pants. The police would find the goods I'd stolen, and my fencers would have to go to no small expense to pay them off. So they said, 'Fakira, doing business with a scaredy cat like you is expensive and dangerous. If some self-righteous cop gets a hold of us, we'll have to do time in jail along with you.' "

"So, Suresh bhajya, I decided if I was going to be a professional, and if this was going to be my profession, I had to get some hard meat on my ass. Now I never tell. I don't even let one word out of my mouth. My attitude now is the bastards can beat me all they want. If I die, they'll be in trouble, too. If I survive, after a month or two of recuperation I'll be on my feet again and back in business."

Fakira said he now had the best reputation in the entire district. His goods sold for the highest prices, and there was never any risk associated with buying or selling them.

Suresh explained to Fakira his own troubles. He said that the burglary would finish his family off for good. His mother, having suffered from diabetes and polio for many years, would die from the shock. Suresh reminded him of their trip to Raipur and told him how she had sung Fakira's praises and blessed him the entire trip. He also said that he had purchased all his things one by one with hard, honest work. He reminded Fakira that even in his current, poor financial condition he was sparing no expense for Fakira's recovery. He thought of Fakira as his brother. Etc., etc.

Fakira polished off the entire orange and kept on smiling at Suresh.

Early the next morning Suresh was on his way to the garage where his truck was being fixed when he saw a sickly-looking man in his early thirties riding a bicycle and singing joyfully the song that was coming from the transistor radio hanging from the handlebars.

bara tera. tera karun din gin-gin ke intazar aja piya ayi bahar

There could be no doubt about it. The transistor hanging from the handlebars of the bicycle was Suresh's.

Suresh ran towards him, and the man on the bicycle, confused, instead of speeding away, put on his brakes. Suresh pounced on the transistor, took hold of it and asked the man where he got it. With no hesitation he said that he bought it at the Gulati Electronics store for a hundred and fifty rupees. By that time a crowd had gathered, including Ashok, Aziz and Lota. The decision was made to go to the Police station. Now there was some hope.

SHO Pandey was wary of getting involved again in this affair. He sent the Head Constable, that is the havaldar, Mishra Gorakhpuriya and two officers to Gulati's store. Suresh went, too. After a few sharp words, Gulati confessed that last week Gopal Rickshewala had sold him that transistor for fifty rupees.

The police knew that Gopal worked for Fakira. Not managing to catch him earned them a month's wages. For small-time cheats and pickpockets they got a week's worth. Another benefit for them in working this way was that they were saved from uselessly having to beat up people.

Pandey, too, became a little excited now. He said to Suresh, "Okay, we'll try it one more time, but you'll have to come along. I don't want to get caught in another mess."

Suresh went with Pandey and three policemen to the slum on the other side of the Railway Colony. In one of those shacks Gopal lived with a twenty-eight year old woman whom he had brought from her village, where she wasn't wanted. When GopaI was away, she carried on her own profession.

Gopal was at home. He did not try to escape. When he saw the police, he knotted up his loongi and came out.

The presence of the police attracted a crowd which, despite Pandey's orders to disperse, did not disperse. GopaI and his companion were both ready for a fight. They verbally abused the mother and sisters of Gulati, of Gulati Electronics. The bastard lies, they said. He traps the poor. Then Gopal and his companion started using lines from the films of Kader Khan and Amitabh Bachchan, which had a tremendous effect on the crowd and gradually brought out a number of Govindas, Mithun Chakrabortys and Anil Kapoors.

The situation was about to become serious when Pandey pulled out his service revolver and roared, "Bastards, I'll see every one of you motherfuckers! Now stop all this Bollywood buk buk and let me get on with my search!"

Then he turned around and said to Gopal's companion "Aren't you a saucy randy. You're showing off all you masala, aren't you? Get inside right now or I'll spank you ass until it steams."

Angrily, she pulled a key chain out of her waist and threw it in his direction. "Go ahead, make your search. In the whole house there's just one tin box. Open it up and have a look. The key chain. Suresh recognized it. His aunt had given it to him when he got married, and she had emphasized the fact that it was pure silver.

"Pandey! That key chain is mine. It's silver."

Aroused, Pandey hit Gopal's companion twice with his stick and went inside with the keys. A cot was in one corner, in another was a kerosene stove and a few pots. A petticoat, was hanging on a line. Too ashamed to admit that it belonged to his wife, Suresh remained silent.

The box was opened. It contained a shawl, four Banarasi sarees, three cotton Kota sarees, a watch, a purse and a George-the-Fifth gold guinea. All of it belonged to Suresh.

When they returned to the station, Pandey told Suresh that in order to make a claim for the confiscation and recovery of his things, they would have to remain in the hands of the police, and they would have to be properly and officially identified. That will take some time, so the best thing to do, he said, "is for you to leave a few sarees here with us. The rest of the things just go ahead and take home."

Suresh added up the value of what had been found. Out of everything that had been stolen it amounted to only ten or twelve thousand rupees. And because of the legal red tape, who knows when he would see it all. The fluttering loincloth of a galloping ghost.

Pandey assured him, though, that now they had a real clue. Gopal wasn't tough like Fakira. He was soft and liked the girls. His companion had him under her thumb and twisted around her little finger. He could probably stand his own beating, but he won't be able to endure hers. He'll spill the beans, all of them.

Suresh again had hope. He left one silk saree and the purse in the hands of the Police and took the rest of the stuff home.

The next night Suresh was eating meat and drinking with his friend and neighbor Amrik Singh, when Amrik, full of liquor, suddenly told him that they knew where his VCR, TV and gold jewelry were. A typhoon of joy swept Suresh away, and he downed a whole peg of rum in one swallow. Almost one hundred thousand rupees of stuff found! The jewelry had caused him the most worry, the hereditary jewelry of his mother and the jewelry that had been a part of Rajshri's dowry.

Amirik was the owner of sixteen trucks and the thriving Amrik Transport Company. He had work to do every day for the Police and various governmental departments. He was the friend, financier and bodyguard for the District MLA, Lakhauri Ram Agrawal, who had now become the State's Minister of Justice and the Minister of Finance and Revenue. Amrik Singh's number two work alone, hauling black market goods, stolen coal and steel girders, and doing bogus contracting for the PWD, earned him hundreds of thousands of rupees.

Amrik said, "Just wait three days, my friend. Every single thing'll come back. So let's celebrate!"

That night they both got dead drunk.

Four days passed. A week. The next week his wife and mother were due to come back from Raipur with the baby. He received no information from the Police, nor did Amrik bring up again what he had mentioned that night. In fact after that celebration Amrik was obviously avoiding him.

Suresh sensed something was up, so one day he himself collared Amrik and asked him about his stolen property "Really?" Amrik said with amazement. "I told you that? Are you sure? Must have been the rum. Nowadays you never know what's in those bottles. It knocks you flat right away. There's no telling what chemicals and junk the mother fuckers mix into it. Forget it friend. Stolen property never comes back."

Suresh could easily see that Amrik Singh was hiding something. The Police had probably held up one of his jobs. To get it through he was using Suresh's stolen goods as a shield, and now he was denying it.

Suresh had one trump card left, Amrik Singh's wife Harpreet. Amrik had, in a way, abandoned her. In the city he had three companions. One was on the joint payroll of Amrik and the State's Minister of Justice and the Minister of Finance and Revenue Lakhauri Ram Agrawal, who had previously been the authorized liquor contractor. She was famous throughout the city as "The Shared Hearth". She, too, drove a Maruti.

Since Harpreet was ignored by her husband, Suresh got to work. Two days later, after a little insistence, some effort and the application of a little bit of intelligence, he got Harpreet to come into his house in the afternoon by means of the back door.

Love and affection filled the room for two or three hours, and during that time he learned from Harpreet that Gopal Rickshewala had in fact told the Police where Suresh's gold jewelry and other stolen goods were. The problem was that they had already reached someone high up.

Fakira had sold all of Suresh's things at a reasonable price to the wife of Mr. Manoharlal Gupta, the CMO (Chief Municipal Officer). She was the sister of Lakhauri Ram Agrawal, the Minister of Justice and the Minister of Finance and Revenue. When the Police found out who had the stolen goods, they naturally backed off. So SHO Pandey went and had a talk with the CMO. Pandey was due a promotion for the past three years, and one of Amrik's contracts had been held up by the Municipality. With Suresh's stolen goods as a shield, both jobs got done.

Suresh became angry. Embracing Harpreet, he lay her beneath him and said, "I'll go over their heads. Who do they think I am? Even an old friend and neighbor like Amrik has turned out to be a liar and a cheat. What's the world come to?"

Closing her eyes in ecstasy, Harpreet said, "And you, Suresh, what duty are you fulfilling now, hmm? What are you doing to Amrik now? Tell me that."

Problems, neglect and her husband's abuse had educated Harpreet to the ways of the world. She said, "Suresh, you're so naive. What a bholay baba. Look, first of all a confrontation with CMO Gupta and Minister Agrawal is not something to take lightly. It's dangerous. The second thing is there is no piece of jewelry now anywhere in the world that looks like the jewelry you described for the Police Burglary Report, having so many stones of such and such a kind. Pandey will have told the CMO to tell his wife that within the next few days she should have that jewelry melted down, just in case there's any trouble. Then, if something does happen, Pandey told him, it won't be your job but mine that'll be in jeopardy."

Enjoying the ecstasy that was lingering throughout her body, Harpreet said, "Bholay baba. Your wife's jewelry no longer exists. All that's left are gold biscuits."

When she was about to leave, she said, "The wise thing for you to do in this case is leave it alone. You cause any more trouble, and I've heard what Pandey and my husband have discussed. You might have an accident. It's water over the dam. Let it go. Whatever enjoyment you can get out of your life to come, take it."

"Oh, yeah, your wife's gold mangala sutra, that she kept safe at home while wearing a fake one; it's safe and sound. The CMO's wife is wearing it, the sister of the Law and Finance Minister. Are you going to be able to go and take it off her?"

Suresh had lost. He was thoroughly defeated and powerless.

Suresh told me this incident in the month of March of this year. It took place, of course, in the external world, outside the literary text. For a long time I have been thinking, and I'm still thinking today, that in order to bring to you this incident that took place totally outside the short story's current form, its root text and language, I will still have to rely on all those conventions which I, you, all of us want to get away from.

For now, however I'm not worried at all about whether this story's language, structure or style is artistically poor or excellent. What concerns me is our society can be so structured that the gold stolen by a rickshaw wallah ends up being melted down in the home of the one who is the Minister of Justice and the Minister of Finance and Revenue.

And isn't the fact that we are unable to change the structure of neither this short story nor our society the defeat of us all?

Is it true that both are inevitable?

The Golden Waistchain

At night the darkness in our house was dense. It was thicker and more extensive than in other houses. The walls totally disappeared in it. The air was heavy and close, many smells having melted into it. A number of times I smelled the sweet fragrance of screwpine, even though there wasn't any nearby or even in the entire village. Sometimes the air carried the odor of the fish-filled pond outside our village. Our lungs would fill with the sweat of the fish, our breath would become heavy, and we would feel the moisture all around us.

And, sometimes it so happened that the smell of something rotten covered the whole house like a fine, thin film. As the odor wafted from place to place, the shadow of an invisible fear also stretched over the house. Mother would say, "It seems a rat died somewhere." Her voice expressed both uncertainty and fear. Then, gradually reassuring herself, she'd say, "Go look in the darkroom and see what Dadi's doing."

I knew that rotten odor darkened Mother's heart with fear, and she became anxious about Dadi. All of us often forgot about her, and sometimes we didn't see her for months. When she wasn't before our eyes, we didn't remember she existed.

The little room in which Dadi slept on an old sheesham cot had been named "the darkroom". It was a very small, narrow, dark room below ground level and without a single window. It had only one small door that was so low one almost had to sit in order to go down into the room. The floor of the room was at least a foot below ground level. The room was always dark, even during the day. Dadi would not leave that room for a number of days at a time or sometimes months. She probably urinated in a corner of the room because its dense, trapped air bore the sharp smell of ammonia. That same smell also came from Dadi's body.

I fully believed that Dadi could see everything in the darkroom very well. Once or twice, when Mother was frightened by that rotting smell and sent me to check on Dadi, I looked inside the darkroom and saw two bluish eyes where Dadi's cot was, glowing in the dark like cat's eyes. When I called out, "Dadi! Oh Dadi!" the sound hoon growled out from the very place where those eyes were.

If, after running back through the darkness, I had proclaimed, "Mother, Dadi is alive", she would have scolded me fiercely. If I had said, "Mother, it's not Dadi that's rotting away; this awful smell must be from something else that's died", she still would have probably scolded me. So those days, when that odor filled the house at night and Mother was totally scared and sent me to the darkroom and I looked in and came running back, I reported in a sing-song manner, "Dadi said, 'Hoon!"

But at night cats would petrify me. Especially the black one, who only came at night, jumped down from the thatch roof, wandered throughout the house, and sometimes sat under my cot. Its eyes, too, were blue and shiny. They emitted a soft, deep yellow light. The thicker the darkness, the more brightly they shone. At night the cat would cry and I would feel it wasn't really a cat but Dadi herself. Maybe that's the form she assumed when she came out to inspect the house. The women of our village told many such stories in which some women became adept at spells and magic and could transform themselves into anything. Women who could do that were called *tohni* and the cat was their favorite form because cats can see in the dark.

But those days not only was Dadi a source of wonder for me, all women were. I was constantly on guard for the chance to see a woman change into something else. But I was never able to do so. I wasn't even able to find out when Dadi changed into a cat.

Auntie, about whom it was said that in the place of her heart was a square wooden block that she had had put there when her husband ran away and she was unable to have children, was very mean. She even cursed. Once she explained that many years ago, when Dadi was young and very pretty, she became familiar with the barber's wife in the village. The barber's wife knew spells and sorcery, and from her Dadi learned a little. On some people, though, spells work in reverse. That's what happened to Dadi. Her beautiful body, which would blister as soon as it was exposed to the sun and on warm summer nights gave off the fragrance of jasmine, first took on the color of copper and then catechu because of a spell that backfired. One after the other, she had thirteen children, of whom only Father, Jasidih wali Auntie and Uncle were still living. Auntie explained that Dadi's use of only partially understood spells was what ate up her children. The effect of her sorcery was what prevented Father and Uncle from being able to stay at home.

Our house was a weak, ill and slowly dying one. In every piece of wood that supported the thatch roof, in every beam, rafter and strut, lived woodworms that rained white sawdust on the floor all day long. Throughout the day sawdust gathered on everything. In the evening Mother swept, forming a pile of sawdust, dust and brick powder in a corner of the courtyard.

Mother knew the walls of the house had already become hollow and in them existed another life and world. It was a world of rats, strange bugs of many colors, and invisible creatures we would never be able to see. It had its own separate code of laws. Our world outside was a sort of fertiliser and air for that other, inner world. We all knew the house was falling apart. Anytime it could suddenly be finished. At night, when there was total silence everywhere and our house was drowning in the air heavy with the pungent smell of fish sweat, a peculiar, thin sound from the world within the walls could be heard. It seemed someone was softly whispering in some totally unfamiliar and unknown language. They were talking about the fate and death of our own external world. The sound of a number of things breaking and being made could be heard. Something new there was being created and formed. Sometimes it seemed that in the hollow of all the walls of the house, from here all the way to there, a huge python was sleeping, whose burning, steamy breath reached into our breath and dreams.

I wasn't only afraid of cats, Dadi and spells, I was also afraid of our house's walls. I believed that if I stood next to a wall and put my ear up against it, I would learn many of the secrets of that other world. But even just thinking that made my heart pound violently. I was unable to muster the courage to listen to that peculiar, unknown and invisible language, the language of that other world. I felt that if I were to hear even one word of it, and if I were to understand it, I would die on the spot.

But I figured Dadi not only knew that language, many of the events in that world occurred because of her bidding. Wrapped around her fingers were the ends of the invisible strings behind every disaster and accident that brought our house closer to destruction. After all, what did she do in the darkroom day and night for months at a time? Dadi was our house's enemy. And she knew it, which was all the same to us. She also knew that except for Raamay (my father) no one could understand a word she said. She was at least eighty years old and totally engrossed in a game or spell that would bring about the end of our house along with her. Because of her spell our house, too, seemed at least eighty years old, and all of us felt our lungs and bones were eighty years old. We wanted to be saved from destruction.

Dadi ate only once a day. In an ancient, dented plate made of zinc, Mother put rice, lentils, chutney and a dried pepper and left it on the threshold of the darkroom. Many, many times, though, even for a number of days in a row, the plate came back every day without having been touched; but no one else ate her food. A number of times we completely forgot Dadi. Not a word was said about her. Months would pass like that. Then one day we'd notice her wearing her dirty white saree, sitting on the garbage pile in a corner of the courtyard, her forehead in her hands. No sooner would Auntie see her than she'd say, "She's come out again today, the old lady. In this house somebody's going to get sick for sure."

As soon as Dadi emerged, a strange agitation and commotion filled the house. Auntie kept up her muttering, stomping the ground loudly, Jasidih wali Auntie removed herself from Dadi's shadow. Mother began sweeping out the entire house, flinging old rags and broken things out into the courtyard. Everyone pretended not to see Dadi. But I knew very well it was the emergence of Dadi that caused the whole house to tremble from within, like a cup brimming with water. Only because of Dadi was everyone busy. The voices of Auntie, Mother and Jasidih wali Auntie became louder. I knew none of this was just for show; it was a manifestation of everyone's hatred and loathing for Dadi. No sooner would Dadi come out of her room than the entire house would start pitching like a boat on the waves, and everyone would gather together like an army against Dadi.

Having covered the garbage pile with a gunny sack, Dadi would remain sitting there. Sometimes she would be seen sewing a small bag, Once, when she caught me staring at her, I saw all the wrinkles of her face contract and transform into a helpless laugh. She motioned for me to come to her. That was Dadi's one and only response to the outside world. Perhaps she was unable to thread her needle. But I didn't go to her because I was afraid she'd stick one of her magic hairs into me without me noticing. Once Auntie told me that tohni women do that sometimes. Then later, they call that hair back with a spell, and when it's put in a bowl of milk, the milk turns into blood, the blood of the little boy that magic hair had absorbed and brought with it. That's why I was afraid. If something like that happened to me, my body would become as white as paper.

Dadi looked like some old vulture, the soft hair of whose head and neck had fallen off and all that was left was a scrawny, sickly, wrinkle-filled neck and a bald skull. The brain inside that skull slowly kept hearing all the sounds of its final moment. I felt some pity for Dadi, but she was our enemy because somewhere–in the floor, in a wall, near the back well, or underneath a nearby tree–she had buried her solid gold waistchain that weighed fifty-six tolas.

At night, when all the housework was finished, Auntie, Mother and Jasidih wali Auntie sat together by the lantern. That was the only lantern in the house. After everyone else had eaten and she had finished the dishes, Mother would eat. She took her food and sat by the lantern. She carefully inspected every mouthful of bread, always pulled something or other out of it, and chewed it slowly and deliberately. Between chews she kept talking. Jasidih wali Auntie was called that because she had been married to someone in Jasidih, near Orissa, and a year later, after her husband died, she returned to our house. Since then, for the past ten years, she's lived here. She expressed everything with astonishment, so her eyes were always wide open. Looking at her, it seemed the entire world was a source of amazement for her, every little thing a secret.

Auntie was very thin and short of stature. She was around fifty years old, and so far her womb remained empty. She had had a square block of wood fixed in place of her heart, so she was mean. Once, she burned my arm with a hot ladle, which caused a big fight with Mother. Maybe it was then that Mother told me about the square block of wood.

The dirty light of the lantern was very weak compared to the darkness that permeated the house. At night all kinds of things submerged into the heavy air, mysterious odors and strange sounds. The world in the hollow of the walls came alive, and the sound of the invisible goings-on there reached us. We all huddled together around the lantern. The conversations that took place among Auntie, Mother and Jasidih wali Auntie were endless and seemed like the dialogue of some immense story. I listened silently and thought that when I grew up I'd write a story about this house for sure.

A morsel of food filled Mother's mouth, in the smoky light of the lantern her face seemed very old, decrepit and unhealthy, and she said, "If Maji gives us that waistchain, this house can still be saved." Auntie said, "Listen to me. When the old lady dies, it'll come out of her guts. She'll never tell us while she's alive." Mother's face went black, and she said, "May God never afflict someone so much that he no longer belongs to anyone." Jasidih wali Auntie often sat quietly. I was amazed that Dadi was her mother. It seemed Dadi had forgotten everyone, even Jasidih wali Auntie, Raamay and Uncle. This whole world was unfamiliar and unknown to her. Now perhaps she was able to use only the magical language of the world within the walls. She had forgotten our language; that's why no one could understand her.

Father was the only one who spent time in the darkroom with Dadi, always an hour or two the day he would return after spending three or four months in Calcutta. They would talk. Dadi was his mother. She was the one who had given birth to him.

That golden waistchain of fifty-six tolas Grandfather had brought. Grandfather was the hero of the story of our house. He had travelled over the entire world and accomplished amazing feats. It seemed to me the whole world must have known about him. A faded photo of him hung in Mother's room. It was the only photograph in the house; it was stuck to the glass, and the humidity and the effects of time were slowly destroying it. Grandfather wore a Marathi turban, a gun was held between his legs, and he had a huge moustache.

In the light of the lantern, whenever the golden waistchain was mentioned, Grandfather's story was always begun. Mother would explain how much Grandfather liked to raise birds. He knew every duck in the village pond and called each one by its own name. Many of them he brought to the house. Then the entire house was full of ducks. Ducks everywhere! What a problem! Grandfather always knew which bird nested on which branch of which tree and how big its young were. Not only ducks, he could also talk with crows and oxen. A number of times he talked with the ants, and he could always tell from them whether or not it would rain.

In that same pond where all Grandfather's ducks, coots, waterhens, lapwings, herons and who knows how many other kinds of birds lived, the Angrez Officer would come with his fair Mem Saheb and shoot ducks with his twelve–gauge shotgun. Sometimes Grandfather would return from his pond in despair and mutter, "Today the white man murdered Mohan, Saawant and Doojee."

Mother explained that one evening Grandfather was lying quietly on his cot in the courtyard, looking up at the Big Dipper, the North Star and Venus, which were then rising, when birds suddenly filled the bluish-orange sky. Birds from all over had gone crazy and were screeching through the air. A waterhen fell on Grandfather's foot. She was covered in blood, her body was full of buck shot, and her neck was half slit. Grandfather cleaned out the bore of his gun, filled it with bullets, put on his turban and headed for the pond.

Then they say that Grandfather stood on the other shore of the pond and told the Angrez Officer it was a crime to kill the birds of that pond. "They're all my pets and domestic fowl," Grandfather said, "so don't come here again for hunting." That day the Angrez Officer was hunting alone, so he left silently with his Mem Saheb. But the next day all Grandfather's fields were confiscated, his cattle were led away, and our village was declared a rebel village.

Now the Angrez Officer came to the pond every evening and hunted the birds with his twelve-gauge shotgun. Grandfather lay quietly on his cot in the courtyard and watched the sky fill with birds–bloody guinea hens, wounded ducks, screaming lapwings and frightened herons. Mother said that the day the Angrez Officer went mad with anger and started firing off his shotgun at the pond's ducks was the same day that shots were fired in Jallianwala Bagh in Punjab.

One day Grandfather again cleaned his gun, went to the other side of the pond, climbed a mango tree and hid among its leaves. The Angrez Officer arrived with his Mem Sabeb and subordinates. He took his position on a platform built in a mango tree. From the other side Grandfather hollered out to him, "From now on it's all over, Lat Saheb! I am the Malik of this pond and of these birds, and I order you..." But in the mango tree Grandfather was invisible. Neither the Officer nor his subordinates could see him. They all supposed it was just their inner fear talking. The Officer became angry. At that time the English ruled over all of Hindustan, and here Grandfather's voice rose up against him for hunting ducks!

From his platform the Angrez Officer aimed at a flock of waterhen; bang! his gun went off, and his subordinates saw the whole sky fill with screaming birds. But then they saw come tumbling out of the sky not a dead bird but the dead body of the Angrez Officer.

Actually, two triggers had been pulled at exactly the same time. Grandfather came down the high bank on the other side of the pond, cleaned the bore of his gun, looked at the birds and smiled, and then he waved his hand and disappeared. Mother said that for twenty-five years after that no one knew where Grandfather was. Some said he became a sadhoo, others a dakoo. All our land was confiscated. Food became hard to get. Alone in the house Dadi raised the three children–Father, Uncle and Jasidih wali Auntie. During that time thousands of stories about Grandfather spread from house to house. Grandfather went to Germany, then to Russia. He swam the oceans and drilled holes in the hulls of English vessels. He became a train robber. Some said he was killed in a fist fight, he was hung, or he died of cancer.

But after twenty-five years, on a Thursday evening, in the month of Kartik, just one day before Diwali, Grandfather returned. He had become very old and thin. He had a white beard, his head was bald. And people say that on the night of Diwali he gave Dadi a waistchain weighing fifty-six tolas, pure gold.

India got her freedom the same year Grandfather returned, but from then on he was ill. They say that when Grandfather was strong, he once stopped a moving train engine all by himself and pushed it back a mile and a half; but after Independence he couldn't even lift the lota he filled with water when he went out to defecate. He had tuberculosis and was always short of breath. By then Father, Uncle and Jasidih wali Auntie themselves had grown up. Jasidih wali Auntie said that the year Independence came, all the people who fought the British got sick and started dying. Grandfather, too, died that same year. During his last days flies covered his face, which was greasy like a ball of brown sugar. He, too, started looking like an old vulture, and he forgot the language of the birds. The day he returned home, he went to his pond, but none of the ducks there recognized him. All the old ducks had died, and for this new generation Grandfather was a complete stranger. He was crushed. All he said was, "Everything's changed." In our upstairs storage room was his brass lota he used for cleaning himself after defecating, and I couldn't even lift it.

In that sickly yellow light of the lantern the faces of Auntie, Mother, Jasidih wali Auntie, of everyone, looked like faded photographs in some old, worm-eaten book. In that air pungent with fish sweat their voices carried only a little distance before they became heavy with moisture and sank. We all knew our house was slowly turning to dust. Mother, too, was becoming dust. Father was able to come only two or three times a year. He worked in Calcutta as an accountant in some Marwari's textile store. Uncle used to come, but for four years we hadn't seen him. Occasionally, a fifty rupee money order came from him.

One day Jasidih waii Auntie and Mother were talking to each other about Uncle in Gauhati and that an Assamese vegetable wali was now living with him. She was very beautiful and knew spells. Whenever Uncle thought about coming home, she turned him into an ox and tethered him to a stake. Jasidih wali Auntie said that if Auntie had had children, Uncle would surely come home. After all, Father comes home, said my mother. Once he even talked about taking me to Calcutta with him, but he just didn't have any room there. He'd been sleeping in the back of the Marwari's store for twelve years.

Once, Father too asked Dadi about her waistchain of fifty-six tolas, and she remained silent for a long time. Then she said, "Raamay, when your father killed the firangi and disappeared, I had ten tolas of gold. I don't know how I managed to raise my three kids and educate you two boys. Four tolas were left, which I distributed equally to the two daughters-in-law. And now, after I did all that, son, you've all gotten together against me, which not only God surely knows, but the whole village." Dadi started crying, then she said, "Now, son, my daughter-in-law brings me my food, but if I give you the waistchain, what hope would be left? Whether there is one or not, son, I need it, and all of you need it to have hope."

Uncle and Father searched through the entire house. An astrologer was consulted, many spots were dug up and the dirt hauled out, but it was impossible to divine where Dadi had hidden her waistchain. Once, Mother saw it in a dream, inside the platform that held the tulsi bush, among the bricks, in a bronze pot and guarded by three white snakes. The platform was ripped apart. Once, on the festival of the third lunar day of the month of Saawan, Dadi was brought out of the darkroom into the courtyard on her cot. Jasidih wali Auntie rubbed her down with mustard oil. Dadi's hair was combed and done up in a bun. Mother fed her halwa, rice pudding, alu-gobhi and poories. She was fanned. Jasidih wali Auntie, Mother and Auntie used every conversational stratagem they could think of to get the secret out of her. Meanwhile, Father dug up every inch of the floor of the darkroom with a crowbar, but the waistchain wasn't there.

Once, Dadi had a high fever. For many days she didn't leave the darkroom. All she did was moan. In place of Auntie's heart was a square block of wood, so she said, "Now's the time. If the old lady's going to tell us, she'll tell us, otherwise who knows when she might breathe her last." So, they say, Auntie frightened and threatened Dadi even when she was sick. She brandished a knife in front of her, strangled her, and closed her nose and mouth for a long time. Unable to breathe, Dadi's body blew up like a balloon, but even then she didn't tell where her waistchain was. Once, for an entire month Dadi wasn't given even one grain of food. Mother, Auntie and Jasidih wali Auntie stood by the door of the darkroom, called out to Dadi and told her the state of the house had become so bad it was necessary now to sell even its bricks, no one had food, Raamay had stopped sending money. No one can take gold to heaven. Yamadoot will take it away from you on the way and feed it to his buffalo, or it'll stay right here. Gold unused while a child dies of hunger turns into shit. "White ants consume it..."

Who knows if Dadi heard all that or not. She was our enemy. Sometimes Father would get angry and say to Mother, "All you people made Maji into an enemy. I'm afraid what'll happen to me in this house when I get old and sick. Maybe I should make it clear now that I have no money. I've given everything I have to support all of you, have some mercy..." One day Father said, "There's no waistchain-chastechain anywhere. It's all in your heads. My father didn't go to Rangoon or Germany. I found out he worked in a brick furnace in Calcutta. Ma used tobacco since the day she was born. And that's the kind of addiction that if she had a golden waistchain, she would have sold it to get tobacco. It's all a lie, there's no waistchain anywhere."

Mother cried late into the night. Then she continued crying for a number of days, while cooking, washing the dishes, sweeping. She was afraid. The only way our house could be saved from destruction, from being reduced to dust, was by the miracle of the golden waistchain of fifty-six tolas. Father's body had started talking back with aches and pains. If there were no waistchain, then the dirt and dust of the years, the woodworms and the mysterious world in the hollow of the walls would turn our house into a pile of old dust, with the bones of all of us at the bottom.

That time, when Father said the waistchain was just imaginary, Mother cried for twenty-five days straight, and for twenty-five days Auntie put dirt and dust in Dadi's food. Father returned to Calcutta the same night he had said the waistchain was imaginary, and for twenty-five nights a darkness filled the house that was thicker and blacker than coal. The lantern would sputter and go out. In the air was always the rotten smell of something that had died. One day Mother sent me to look in the darkroom, and there I saw Dadi's bluish eyes glowing in the dark, and I heard her moaning. The air was sharp with the smell of urine. On the threshold was the dented up zinc plate with its rice and lentils in which Auntie had mixed dirt and dust. A terrible war had broken out in our house. Dadi was on one side, and the entire house was on the other. Where I was, was not clear. All night the black cat wandered through the house, in every corner.

All day the woodworms rained sawdust down from the thatch roof, and everything was covered with dirt and dust. When we woke up in the morning, the sawdust covered our sheets, our hair and our eyebrows. During the day Mother, Auntie, Jasidih wali Auntie, all of them swept a number of times. The pile of dust, sawdust and brick powder in the corner of the courtyard got very high. Then one day Grandfather's photograph in Mother's room fell all by itself, and everyone saw with fear and amazement that Grandfather's face wasn't in the frame. Instead were a number of insects of all sizes, their backs shiny and golden. They had also eaten up the wood of the frame. In the upstairs storage room I saw that Grandfather's lota was gone.

The village women said Dadi's sons, daughters and daughters-in-law had put her in the worst of all hells. Before anyone has to endure old age like that, they said, God, should take him away.

I had another memory of Dadi, from many years ago. Then, the war in our house hadn't reached its present ferocity, and Dadi wasn't so old. One day she pulled out of her little bag a wooden elephant on wheels and a rubber ball and gave them to me. She used to sing devotional songs, which were hard to understand : *haaya dita raam... haaya dita raam*...But that was a long time ago. That Dadi has nothing in common with the Dadi of today. Dadi now has completely forgotten who I am. Maybe she had decided I was her enemy, too, and tossed me out of her memory on purpose. She didn't remember anyone. She didn't even remember our language.

Before, Dadi never ate rice. She was from the North. If rice was made for Grandfather, Dadi would still make some rotis separately for herself. But now, whenever I saw the zinc plate at her door, it always held rice. Tobacco, too, she hadn't been able to enjoy for years. Nothing she used to enjoy was left for her in this world. Even if there was something somewhere, Dadi was unable to get her hands on it. In war everything's permissible. On Dadi every weapon was used. And she, too, used all her magic and sorcery in her effort to destroy our house. Sometimes it seemed Dadi was about to be defeated and she would soon take out her golden waistchain of fifty-six tolas and fling it into the courtyard, the war would be over; but then it looked like Dadi was winning. She made our house hollow and decrepit inside. Her army–the darkness, the cat, the air, the woodworms, the rats, illness and bad news–fought for her valiantly. Jasidih wali Auntie's husband died, the Assamese vegetable wali turned Uncle into an ox and kept him tied to a stake, Father was unable to come home for months at a time, Auntie remained barren, the rain didn't fall. Our four fields were sold off. The remaining land at the back was mortgaged off. Grandfather's bronze lota had been sold, and his photograph bright bugs had eaten up. Dadi was winning the war.

That day, in the evening, Dadi came out of the darkroom. For the past ten days Auntie had not allowed her to be given any food. Dadi looked like an ill, yet mobile, skeleton, and her body gave off the odor of urine. She sat on the heap of garbage, without spreading a gunny sack over it. Her skull was bare. Not a hair on it. Beneath it was a long, scrawny neck, full of wrinkles. Her eyeballs had sunk into their hollows, and they seemed not to be looking out but in.

Fixed on her skinny neck, Dadi's bare skull was trembling, and water was coming out of the hollows of her eyes. Her whole body was trembling. Her hands were shaking in the air like leaves.

I saw that Jasidih wali Auntie got scared when she saw Dadi. Then she said to Mother, "It looks like Mother's got malaria. She's shaking with fever." Mother looked out the kitchen window at Dadi. Sitting like a sick, old vulture on the garbage pile in the comer of the courtyard, feverish, Dadi was singing, "*Haaya dita raam...haaya dita raam...*"

Auntie said, "This time the old lady won't survive. Be careful, or everything'll be ruined. This is our last chance. If the old lady gives it to us now, then she gives it; if not, we're finished." I saw Auntie go over to Dadi. She lifted her up off the garbage, grabbing her by the arm. Dadi's slight arms were just bones covered by a thin, ancient skin full of shiny scabs and wrinkles. She kept on singing, "*Haaya dita raam...bina dhaji ka painaa do/ata hai...bina dhaji ka painaa do/ata hai... haaya dita raam...*"

Auntie put her mouth up against Dadi's ear and shouted "Oh, Maji, a telegram came from your son! He's very sick! Three pounds of gallstones are stuck in his belly! He has no money for the operation! Maji, tell us where the waistchain is, or your son will die!" Then Mother, too, came. She also grabbed Dadi. And she screamed in her ear, "Maji; Raamay won't survive! Your little grandson is sick, too! And he won't survive either! Give us the waistchain!"

But clearly, Dadi had forgotten a long time ago the language of this world. Her bare skull kept on trembling, the water kept coming out of the deep hollows in which her eyeballs had retreated, her hands kept shaking like dry leaves, and from her toothless mouth she kept on singing, "Haaya dita raam...haaya dita raam..." Then she had a fit, and fell unconscious.

Just then Auntie screamed, "Bahanji, look underneath her! I think Maji's having diarrhea." Yes, the dirty saree under Dadi was smeared with diarrhea, and the stinking yellow mass was oozing out onto the courtyard. Then her body gave off the sharp smell of urine. The whole house reeked with the stench of shit and piss. I was about to throw up. Dadi's skeleton, smeared with diarrhea, kept trembling because of her fever. *Haaya dita raam...haaya dita raam.*

Jasidih wali Auntie brought a bucket full of water, and Auntie dumped it all out on Dadi's head. Dadi's dirty saree stuck to her bones. The water, diarrhea and urine became mud in the courtyard. The stench became even worse. Auntie kept screeching in Dadi's ear, "Maji, can you hear?! Your son won't survive! Your grandson, too, will die! Take it out now! And give it to us! Oh, Maji...!"

A second bucket, a third bucket, then a fourth bucket of water was poured on Dadi's head. It looked like her skeleton was trembling less. Her head was rolling back and forth. Her singing had stopped. Supported by Mother and Auntie, she was taken back to the darkroom, but no one could stay there. The darkroom, too, reeked of diarrhea and urine.

Auntie said, "The old lady'll change her clothes herself. Didn't you see what strength she still has in those old bones. She wouldn't even let the two of us hold her up. The old lady must have taken some longevity potion; she won't go so easily." For the first time I saw Jasidih wali Auntie's face sad and dark. She said, "But this time she seemed much worse. Maji never did that before."

That night the black cat didn't appear. The lantern gave off a brighter glow than usual. In the air there was no stink, no pungent smell of fish sweat. Once or twice I even sensed the sweet fragrance of jasmine. It was a pleasant night, that felt as light as paper. The world inside the walls went to sleep. Mother, Jasidih wali Auntie and Auntie kept on talking, and I fell asleep. I had a long, deep sleep.

The next morning Auntie came running into the courtyard. Her face had lost all its color. Standing in the middle of the courtyard, she yelled to Mother, "Bahanji, come out, quick! Maji's died! I just looked in the darkroom!"

Mother left her pots and came out into the courtyard. She had just put a pot of water on the hearth. Then Jasidih wali Auntie started crying. A little later all three of them were crying in unison. Almost like music. Then the village women started coming. The courtyard became full. The whole house resonated with the grieving of the women. I was crying and surreptitiously wondering whether or not, out of all these women, one of them could change all by herself into something else. I couldn't get up the courage to go toward the darkroom, even though just once I wanted to stand by the doorway and look in. Who knows, maybe Dadi's bluish eyes would still be glowing, and when I called to her, she'd roar out, "hoon!" Just once I wanted to see the zinc plate in which Dadi got her food that Auntie had adulterated with dirt and dust.

By the afternoon Dadi had been burned on the shore of the pond. That night again the darkness wasn't as thick as usual. The fragrance of screwpine even was in the air. The python inside the wall wasn't breathing. But a few times I had the mistaken sensation that I could hear Dadi's frail, tiny voice singing *haaya dita raam...haaya dita raam...*

On the seventh day Father came. Uncle, too, had been sent a telegram, but he neither responded nor came. The Assamese vegetable wali, after all, had turned him into an ox.

The evening of Dadi's tenth day Father entered the darkroom. The things in her little basket were barely identifiable. Along with four or five dried-out, black guavas was a black wooden ball which many years ago must have been rubber. In a small bag was a wooden horse, with wheels, that had turned into coal. In another small basket were two clumps of brown sugar that had turned into clay. Other than that there were just some torn rags. That was all Dadi had possessed.

Auntie swept out the darkroom well. Dadi's cot was thrown into the pond (and the Dom probably pulled it out). With his crowbar Father dug into the walls and floor of the darkroom. Mother began muttering the thousand Names of Lakshmi so that the waistchain would turn up. Jasidih wali Auntie hauled the dirt out of the darkroom with a shallow pan and threw it outside. The sound of Father's crowbar didn't let up. Black henbane seeds and incense burned throughout the house. Auntie sat me in her lap and said, "Now everything's going to be fine. The sins of the house have gone away. You'll see, we'll find the waistchain now."

Meaning, Dadi's sorcery was coming to an end. Dadi had died, and we were on the verge of winning. Now our house won't turn into dust. All the thatch will be replaced. The hollow walls will be filled with mortar and cement. We'll get our four fields back. Father will be able to give up his job in Calcutta and stay at home. The land in the back will once again be ours; Uncle will return from Gauhati, and the Assamese vegetable wali will work in our kitchen and in our fields; I'll start going to school; Mother's illness will become cured; the air will have the fragrance of screwpine, and our house will have many lanterns, and a flashlight...

Mother was reciting louder. Jasidih wali Auntie was hauling the dirt and pieces of broken wall out of the darkroom and throwing them outside. A large pile was forming. Night was falling. Auntie was sitting with me. I don't know when I fell asleep.

In the middle of the night, noise and the sound of crying and wailing suddenly broke my sleep. Mother and Jasidih wali Auntie were crying, desperately. The lantern had been placed in the middle of the courtyard, and in the dirty light piles of bricks, pieces of wall and dirt could be seen all over the courtyard. On the other side was Father, his body trembling. A pickaxe was in his hands. He had dug out the walls and floor of the darkroom, and now in the same way he was digging up the rest of the house. Like a spirit of destruction. Dhup...dhup sounded his pickaxe. I was frightened. I had never seen Father like that before. He was covered with dust and dirt. Each time, the sound hoon came out of his throat, and his pickaxe dug into the house.

Scared, I began crying. Auntie said softly, "I don't know what's come over your father so suddenly. The old lady must have left a curse in the darkroom. When he came out of it, his eyes were red and he'd lost his mind...O God, you're our only protector now..."

Father kept on digging up the house. The lantern was sputtering in the darkness. In the air was the rotten stench of something that had died. Mysterious sounds started coming from the world within the walls. Swift squabbling. Some things were being put together, and some were being taken apart.

I saw that the woodworms in the roof had rained down so much dust that my sheet, hair and eyebrows were covered with it. Auntie, Mother and Jasidih wali Auntie were all covered in sawdust. Dirt and sawdust were filling the floor. The lantern sputtered and went out, and there in the darkroom, from where Father had proceeded to dig up the rest of the house, two bluish eyes were glowing in the darkness.

A little later the black cat began roaming through the house. Intermittently, along with the wailing of Mother and Jasidih wali Auntie, the cat too let out a scream.

Tirich

This incident involves my father, my dream, and the city. It also involves my fear of the city, which I've had since I was born.

At the time, Father was fifty-five years old. His body was thin. His hair was as white as cornsilk. It was as if he had cotton on his head. He thought a lot and spoke very little. When he did speak, we felt relieved, as if a breath had been held for a long time and then released. But at the same time we were afraid. For us, children he was an immense mystery. We knew that he had the strongbox that contained all the knowledge of the world. We knew that he could speak all the languages of the world. The world knew him, and just like us, it feared and respected him.

We were proud to be his offspring.

A few times over the years he would take us out in the evening somewhere for a stroll. Before setting out he would fill his mouth with tobacco. Because of the tobacco he wasn't able to say anything, and that silence seemed to us to be so dignified, wondrous, and profound. When my little sister would sometimes ask him something on the way, I would immediately try to answer her, so that Father wouldn't have to speak.

That was quite a difficult and dangerous business for me. Because I knew that if I gave the wrong answer, then Father would have to speak. And speaking disturbed him. First of all, he'd have to take the plug of tobacco out of his mouth. And then he'd have to leave the world in which he lived and negotiate the long, arduous journey down here to our world. But as it was, my sister never asked anything important. She would ask things like what's the name of that bird over there. Since I knew the names of all the birds, I was able to tell her that that was the blue-necked jay, for instance, and people are supposed to see it on the festival of Dussehra. All my efforts were made so that Father could relax and continue his thinking.

My mother and I both made every effort to keep Father happy and content in his own world. He shouldn't have to be forcibly taken from it. That world was full of mystery for us; nevertheless, even while remaining in his world, he could still solve many problems concerning our house and lives. Like the time there was a problem with my student fees. At that time we didn't even have a glass to drink out of, everyone drank water out of the small metal container we call a lota. Father remained silent for two days. Mother, too, was beginning to wonder if he hadn't completely forgotten about the problem or if it was something totally out of his control. But on the third day, early in the morning, Father gave me an envelope with a letter inside and sent me to the city's Doctor Punt. I was astonished when the doctor gave me a fruit drink, brought me inside and introduced me to his son, and gave me three 100 rupee bills.

We were proud of Father, loved him, feared him, and his presence gave us the feeling that we were living in a fort. A deep moat was all around us, the towers rose very high, the walls were of hard red stones, and our fort was impregnable to any outside attack. Completely carefree, we played and ran around on its ramparts. And at night I always had a sound, sound sleep.

But that day, when Father came back in the evening from a stroll, a bandage was tied to his ankle. A little later, many people from the village came. It became known that a tirich, a poisonous lizard, had bitten him in the jungle.

We all knew it was impossible to survive the bite of a tirich. That night a number of people from the village gathered in the smoky lantern light in our courtyard. Father was sitting on the ground, in the middle of them. Then Chutuwa the barber came from the next village over. He extracted the poison with castor-oil leaves and the ashes of cowdung patties.

I had seen a tirich once.

On the shore of the pond are piles of boulders that get very hot in the afternoon–from a crack in one of them I saw the tirich come out going to the pond to drink.

Thanu was with me. He told me it was a tirich, its poison being a hundred times stronger than a black snake's. He told me that a snake only bites when someone steps on it or when someone teases it a lot, but a tirich will run after you whenever it catches your eye. To get away from it, you should never run in a straight line. You should run in zigzags, spirals, and make random turns.

The truth of the matter is that when a man runs, he doesn't just leave foot-prints behind him on the ground, he also leaves some of his smell there in the dirt where the mark is. The tirich follows you by means of that smell. In order to trick the tirich, Thanu said, a man first has to run quickly for a while, making a lot of footprints very close to each other. Then four or five times he has to take real long leaps. Smelling his way, the tirich will come running. Where the footprints are close together, its speed will be very fast, but when it reaches the part where the leaps occurred, it won't know what to do. It'll wander around here and there till it comes upon the next footprint that is imbued with that smell.

We knew two other facts about the tirich. First, as soon as it bites somebody, it runs away from there and urinates and then rolls around in its urine. If a tirich is able to accomplish all that, the person bitten has no chance of survival. If the person wants to survive, he either has to kill the tirich immediately after being bitten, or he has to immerse himself in a river, well, or pond before the tirich is able to roll around in its urine.

The second fact is that the tirich is only able to bite someone when it has looked directly into that person's eyes. If you see a tirich, then never look directly into its eyes. As soon as it looks into a person's eyes, it knows his smell and starts out after him. Then, even if the person were to wander over the entire earth, the tirich would be able to follow him.

Like all children, I, too, was very scared of the tirich. Only two really dangerous characters appeared in my nightmares, the elephant and the tirich. The elephant, though, would get tired after running a lot, and I could climb a tree to get away from him, or I could fly, but the tirich–confronted by him, a spell would overpower me. In my dream I would be going somewhere, and suddenly it would be there. There was no way to predict where it would be. It didn't have to be in the fissure of a stone, in the rubble of old buildings, or in a bush. I would come across it in the marketplace, the cinema hall, a store, or even in my room.

In my dream I would try to avoid looking in its eyes, but it would look at me so familiarly that I would be unable to stop myself. And that was it. As soon as our eyes met, its expression would change; it would come running and I would flee.

I would make big circles, take a lot of quick steps together and suddenly make huge leaps; I would try to fly, I would climb high places, but despite all I would do, I could never shake it. It was so cunning, knowing, clever and dangerous. I felt it knew me so well! The gleam in its eyes that was so familiar to me made me think that in the tirich I had an enemy that knew every thought of mine as it came to me.

My most disturbing, terrifying, and horrifying dream was when I had run so much that I was tired. I couldn't breathe, I was drenched in sweat and about to lose consciousness, and a frightening, stupefying death was only seconds away. I would scream at the top of my lungs, cry bitterly, and call out for Father, Thanu, or Mother, then I would realize it was a dream. But even so, even knowing full well that this was all just a dream, I still couldn't escape death. Death, what, being murdered by a tirich! And still in my dream I would try to make myself wake up. I would put all my might into it, I would open my eyes wide, I would try to look at the light, and I would say something out loud. Many times, just in the nick of time, I'd succeed in waking up.

Mother would tell me that I had talked and screamed in my sleep. A number of times she had also seen me crying in my sleep. That's when she should have jolted me awake, but she would stroke my forehead, tuck me in with the quilt, and leave me there alone in that terrifying world. So I would scramble, run, and scream in my weak effort to escape death, to escape my murderer.

Gradually, I learned by experience that at such a moment speech was my best weapon. Yet unfortunately, every time, only at the very last moment would I remember that, when it was just at the point of taking me. I would feel myself breathing my last, I would be surrounded by the lifeless, terrifying darkness that reeked of death, I would have no solid foundation beneath me, I would float in the air, and the time would come when my end was near. Just then, at the most fragile of all moments, I would remember that weapon and start talking as loud as possible, and by means of that talking I would emerge out of my nightmare. I would wake up.

Many times Mother would ask me what had happened, but it was impossible for me to find the words to explain to her everything that had occurred. I was completely aware of this inability of mine, and because of that, I was filled with a strange sort of tension, an uncomfortable and helpless feeling. Finally, I'd resort merely to saying to her, "A very bad nightmare."

I don't know why, but I wondered if it wasn't that very same tirich that had bitten Father, the one that I knew, the one of my nightmares.

But one good thing was that Father had chased it right after it had bitten him and had killed it. It was certain that if he hadn't killed it immediately, it would have urinated somewhere and rolled in it. Then there would have been no hope for Father at all. For that reason I wasn't worried at all about Father. And I gradually even began to feel a certain comfort, the joy of relief, inside. First, because Father had immediately killed the tirich, and second because my most dangerous, familiar, old enemy had finally died. He had been destroyed, and now in my dreams I could fearlessly wander wherever I wanted, whistling away.

That night the crowd remained in our courtyard till quite late. Various healing rituals were performed on Father. The wound was cut open and blood was taken out, and the red chemical that's put in the well, potassium permanganate, was put on the wound. I had no worries.

The next morning Father had to go to the city. There was going to be a hearing in court, and he had been summoned. The road by which buses went to the city was about two kilometers away from our village. During the entire day there were at the most two or three buses. It was fortunate that just us Father arrived at the road, a tractor came from a nearby village that was headed for the city. He knew the people on the tractor. It would make it to the city in two or two-and-a-half hours, that is to say, well before the court opened.

On the way the people on the tractor talked about the incident with the tirich. Father showed his ankle to them. Among them was Pundit Ram Avatar. He explained that another important fact about the poison of the tirich was that sometimes it would take effect only twenty-four hours, to the minute, after it had first entered the bloodstream. Therefore, Father still had something to worry about. Others turned Father's attention to a mistake he had made. They said that it was good he had immediately killed the tirich, but then he shouldn't have just left it like that. He should have at least burned it.

They maintained that a lot of worms, insects, and other creatures have the ability to come to life again when moonlight hits them. The dew and coolness that exist in moonlight have the elixir of life in them, and many times it's been observed that a snake that people thought had been killed came to life again and escaped when its body became moist from the moonlight. Then, it would always be ready for a chance to get its revenge.

The people in the tractor wondered if the tirich may not have revived at night. Then it would have urinated somewhere and rolled in it, and if that were the case, then exactly twenty-four hours after its bite, the fatal poison would begin to show its effect on Father. They advised Father that he should go back right away, and if by chance the dead body of the tirich was right there where he had left it, he should burn it thoroughly. But Father told them how important the hearing was. This was his third summons, and if he wasn't present in court this time, he was afraid he'd be arrested without bail. The hearing concerned the very house we lived in. The previous two times the lawyer couldn't be given his fees, and if he begins to get careless, and if the judge just feels like it, he could have our property attachéd.

It was a strange situation. If father were to get down from the tractor to go back to our village and burn the tirich's body, then he would be arrested without bail, and our home would be taken away from us. The court had become our enemy.

But Pundit Ram Avatar was an ayurvedic physician as well as a scholar. In addition to astrology he had a very profound knowledge of roots and herbs. He offered a suggestion by which Father would be able to be present at the hearing and would still be able to escape the twenty-four-hour delayed reaction of the poison of the tirich. Pundit Ram Avatar explained that the essence of the Charaka Samhit was that poison itself was the antidote for poison. If they could get some thorn apple seeds somewhere, those could take care of the venom of the tirich.

In the next village, Samatpur, the tractor was stopped, and after some searching, a thorn apple was found in an oil presser's field. The seeds were ground, boiled up along with an old copper coin, and the extract was ready. It was extremely bitter. So it was mixed up in a cup of tea that was then served to Father. After that, everyone's worries disappeared. An effort had been made to pull Father out of an extremely dangerous situation.

A few hours after Father had left, I suddenly remembered a third fact about the tirich. This fact is similar to the one about snakes, because of which, cameras had been invented.

It is believed that while someone is in the act of killing a snake, at the last moment before it dies, the snake peers very carefully at its murderer's face. The person continues to kill it, and the snake stares intently, recording every little detail of the person's face on the screen inside its eyes. After the snake's death, a clear image of its murderer's face remains inside the snake's eyes.

Later, after the person leaves, the snake's mate comes and stares inside its companion's eyes, and thus it comes to know who the murderer is. All snakes, then, one-by-one learn the image of the murderer from other snakes. Then, wherever he might go, they lie ready to take revenge. Every snake becomes his enemy.

I wondered if Father's face had been recorded inside the eyes of the dead tirich, if another tirich had come by and stared in its eyes, and if it had seen Father's picture there. These thoughts made me wonder uncomfortably why Father hadn't been vigilant in this matter. Along with killing the tirich, he should have taken a stone and smashed its eyes to bits. But what could be done now? Father had already gone to the city, and I was stuck with the problem, the challenge, of finding that spot, in the vast jungle near our village, where Father had killed and left the tirich.

I took some kerosene in a bottle, some matches, and a stick and set out wandering in the jungle with Thanu for the tirich. I would be able to recognize it easily, very easily. Then thought it was hopeless.

Then, I suddenly realized that I knew the place we were in very well. Every tree was familiar to me. Many times in my nightmares I had run to this place to save myself from the tirich. I looked intently in every direction, it was exactly the same place. I told Thanu that a certain distance south of here flowed a rather narrow creek. Over the creek were some big cliffs where a big old acacia tree stood, and in the tree were a number of large beehives. They were so huge they seemed to be many centuries old. I knew the brown color of one of the rocks that remained half-submerged in the stream during the rainy season, and afterwards, when the water level sank, mud filled its crevices and gave root to some very unusual plants. Over the rock grew a layer of green. In the topmost level of that same rock the tirich lived. Thanu attributed all this to my imagination.

Nevertheless, we soon came to that creek, the old acacia tree with the beehives, and the rock as well. The dead body of the tirich was at a little distance from the rock, lying flat on its back in the grass. Without a doubt, this was the same tirich. A thrilling sensation of violence, excitement, and happiness overcame me.

Thanu and I gathered dried leaves and sticks, drenched the tirich and the tinder with kerosene, and lit it. While the tirich was being consumed, the smell of its burning body permeated the air. I wanted to shout for joy, but I was afraid I might wake up and discover that all this was a dream. I looked at Thanu. He was crying. He was my best friend.

In my nightmares the tirich had come out of this very place numerous times and followed me. It's amazing that all this time, despite knowing full well where it came from, during the day I never came and tried to kill it.

That day, I was ecstatically happy.

Pandit Ram Avatar explained that at about 9:45 am the tractor had come to the toll station on the outskirts of the city, and they had to wait a while to pay the toll. There, Father had gotten out of the tractor to urinate. When he returned, he said that he was feeling a little light-headed. About one-and-a-half hours had passed since he had taken the thorn apple extract. Somewhere between 10:05 and 10:07 am the tractor had dropped Father off in the city. Nandalal, the teacher from the village called Pelarah, had been sitting in the tractor, and he said that when Father had gotten out of the tractor at the intersection near the Minerva Cinema, he had complained that his throat felt dry. He had also said that he was a little worried because he didn't know the way to the courthouse, and it was difficult for him to keep on asking the city people as they hurried here and there.

Another problem Father had was that he easily remembered the footpaths in the village and the jungle, but he could never remember one city street from another. He very rarely went to the city. When he did have to go, he always put it off until the very last minute, until it was absolutely necessary. Many times he would set out for the city with all his things, but he would return from the bus station, without having gone. His excuse would be that he had missed the bus, while we all knew that hadn't been the case. Father would have seen the bus, then he would have squatted somewhere, to urinate or to chew paan. Then he would have noticed that the bus was leaving. He would have waited a little longer. When the bus began to speed up, he would have run after it for a while. Then he'd slow down and come back, expressing both sadness and anger. By so doing, he would have even been able to convince himself that he had actually missed the bus. When we would have thought that he had already left for the city, he'd come back and startle us all.

I can only vaguely infer what happened to Father in the city from approximately 10:07 am, when he got out of the tractor at the intersection near Minerva Cinema, directly opposite the Singh Watch Company, and 6:00 pm. What I do know comes from inquiries and conversations with some people who saw him. It doesn't matter who, when anyone dies quite suddenly and in an unnatural manner, it is difficult to get a really complete and truthful account of, in this case, where Father went and what happened to him between 10:10 am and 6:00 pm on Wednesday, May 17, 1972. Those incidents can only be inferred from the information that was gathered afterward.

For example, Nandalal, the teacher from Pelarah, says that Father had complained of a dry throat when he got down from the tractor. Before that, when Father came back from urinating at the toll station, he had mentioned that he felt a little dizzy. The thorn apple seed extract had begun to take effect. Almost two hours had passed from the time Father had drunk the extract till he reached the city. Father must have been very thirsty by then. In order to slake his thirst he must have headed for a restaurant or a diner, but based on what I know of his nature, he would have just stood there for a while and would not have been able to decide to ask for a glass of water. One time he told us how, many years ago, in the summer, when he asked for water at a restaurant, the people working there only cursed at him. Father was a very sensitive person, so he would have borne his thirst and left without drinking.

It was impossible to find out where Father went from 10:15 am to about 11:00 am. Nothing important seems to have happened. It's difficult to say whether or not any of the passersby on the streets saw him or took any notice of him. My own guess is that Father would have asked people the way to the courthouse, and he would have planned that once he got to the courthouse, he would find his lawyer, Mr. S.N. Agrawal, and he would ask him for water. But in response to him people either must have gone on with their busy lives without answering, or if they did answer, they did so with such fury and impetuosity that Father wouldn't have been able to understand, so he would have been insulted, discouraged, upset, and stuck. That's what happens in the city.

My own inference about what happened during those forty-five minutes is that the effect of the extract had become quite strong. The hot May sun and Father's thirst would have made its effect even sharper and deeper. He would have started staggering and it's quite possible that he would have had dizzy spells a few times.

At 11:00 am Father entered the State Bank of India building on Deshbandhu Street. I don't fully understand why he went there. Ramesh Dutt, who is from our village, is a clerk in the Land Development Cooperative Bank in the city. It's possible that Father only remembered that he worked in a bank, and while passing by there, Father suddenly saw the words "State Bank" written, so he went inside. By then he hadn't been able to get a drink, so he must have thought that he would ask Ramesh Dutt for some water, he would ask for directions to the courthouse, he would be able to tell him that his head was spinning a little and that a tirich had bitten him yesterday evening. According to Agnihotri, the State Bank's cashier, he himself was just then checking over the cash registry. A number of bundles, amounting to approximately Rs.18,000, were lying on his desk. It must have been 11:02 or 11:03 when Father came in. His face was covered with dust, he looked frightening, and suddenly he yelled something. Agnihotri says that he immediately got scared. Generally, such people aren't able to penetrate inside the bank as far as the cashier's desk. Agnihotri also says that if he had seen Father coming toward him beforehand, he probably wouldn't have become so frightened. But as it was, he was totally absorbed in working out the cash register's accounts, when suddenly Father let out a noise, Agnihotri lifted his head, saw Father's face, was terrified, and let out a scream. He also sounded the alarm.

According to two attendants, two security guards, and other workers, as soon as they heard the cashier's scream and the alarm bell, everyone was aghast and ran in that direction. Meanwhile, the Nepali security guard Thapa had pounced on Father, struck him, and led him into the common room. One attendant, Ram Kishore, who was about thirty-five years old, said that he thought either a drunk or a crazy had gotten into the bank, and since his duty had been at the bank's main entrance, the Branch Manager could have fired him. But when Father was being hit, he started saying something in English. Because of that, the attendants had some doubts about what they thought had happened. Then it seems that the Assistant Branch Manager Mehta said that this man should be thoroughly searched and then removed from the building. The attendant Ram Kishore recalls Father's face had become unusually frightening. It was packed with dust, and the odor of vomit came from his mouth. The attendants say they didn't beat Father very much, but outside the bank, right near the entrance, is a paan shop, and Bunnu, who was sitting in it then, says that at approximately 11:30 am, when Father came out of the bank, his clothes were torn and his lower lip was cut and bleeding. Beneath his eyes there was swelling and beige-colored blotches, the kind that later become black and blue.

I could get no information at all about where Father went after that, that is, from 11:30 am to 1.00 pm. Bunnu, the paanwallah outside the State Bank, did mention one other thing, but he either wasn't totally certain about it or he refused to say everything he knew because he was afraid of the people who worked in the bank. He explained that when Father came out of the State Bank, perhaps (and he put a lot of emphasis on that word) Father had said that the bank attendants had taken all his money and documents away from him. But Bunnu said that it's possible that Father had said something else because he was unable to speak clearly, his lower lip had been cut badly, spittle was drooling out of his mouth, and he wasn't in his right mind.

My own guess is that by this time the effect of the extract on Father had become even stronger. Pundit Ram Avatar, however, denies that that could have been the case. During Holi people pop thorn apple seeds along with intoxicating hemp, and no one has ever gone totally mad because of it. Pundit Ram Avatar believes that either the poison of the tirich had risen through his body and the madness that causes had penetrated his brain, or, it's quite possible that when Thapa the security guard and the bank's attendants beat him up, he could have suffered an injury to the base of his skull, and he could have lost his mind because of that. I think, however, that even at that time Father was still quite under control and he was making every effort to get out of the city. Perhaps he thought that since his money and papers had been taken from him at the bank, there was no longer any sense in him staying there. Perhaps he also thought a few times that he should return to the State Bank and at least request that his documents be given back. But he didn't have the courage to do that. He must have been afraid. That was the first time in his whole life that he had been beaten like that, so he probably wasn't able to think clearly. He was a very thin man, and his appendix had acted up ever since he was a child. It's also possible that the effect of the extract had become so strong that he was unable to think about any one thing for long, so he was wandering around here and there under the influence of first one thought and then another which flitted in and out of his mind like little birds. But there's one thing I'm certain of. He definitely wanted to get out of the city and return home. That thought was constant, it repeatedly emerged out of the darkness, even though it might have been very weak and dim.

About 1:15 pm Father arrived at the police station which was at the far end of the city, near the war memorial and the circuit house. It's ironic that the courthouse was barely a kilometer from there. If Father had wanted, he could have walked there in ten minutes. What I don't understand is that if Father had come this far, did he still have in mind to go to the courthouse? He no longer had his papers with him.

The S.H.O. of the station, Mr. Raghavendra Pratap Singh, said that at 1:15 pm he had opened the tiffin he had brought from home and was preparing to have lunch. That day he had bitter gourd along with his parathas. He couldn't eat bitter gourd, and he was wondering what he should do, when Father came in. Father didn't have a shirt on, and his pants were torn. It looked like he had either fallen or been hit by a truck. Only one policeman was in the station then, Gajadhar Prasad Sharma. He said that he thought Father was some beggar. He had accosted him, but Father had gone right by him all the way to the S.H.O.'s desk. The S.H.O. said that because of the bitter gourd in his lunch his "mood was off". Despite thirteen years of married life, his wife still hadn't learned what things he didn't like to the extent that he loathed them. He had just put a bite in his mouth when Father came up right next to him. Vomit was on Father's face and chest, and he stank. The S.H.O. asked Father what he wanted, but he couldn't understand Father's answer. S.H.O. Raghavendra Singh regretted the fact that if he had known that the man was the retired headmaster from Bukaylee, he would have allowed him to sit in the station at least for a few hours. He wouldn't have let him go outside. But at the time he thought he was some crazy who had come in because he had seen him eating, so he hollered at the policeman Gajadhar Sharma, who dragged Father out of the station. Gajadhar Sharma says that he didn't hit Father at all, that when Father came to the station, his lower lip was cut, his chin was skinned, and his elbows were all scratched up. He must have fallen somewhere.

No one knew where Father wandered for one-and-a-half hours after he left the police station. It is difficult to determine whether or not he had had a drink of water all day. The possibility of it seems slight. It's possible that by then he had lost control of his mind to such an extent that he could no longer remember that he was thirsty. But since he reached the police station, despite the loss of his faculties, he must have had in mind, however fragilely, to ask how to get back to the village, to ask where he could find that tractor, or to have a report written about the swiping of his money and legal papers. It's quite unsettling to realize all that Father was up against then. Not only was he fighting the poison of the tirich and the thorn apple's appropriation of his mental faculties, but also his mind must have repeatedly awoken out of its drugged sleep because of the worry of how to save our house. Perhaps he had begun thinking that all of this must have been a dream. Father must have been constantly trying both to wake up and to get out.

Around 2:15 pm Father was seen dragging himself around in Itawari Colony, the most affluent neighborhood, in the most northerly area of the city. It was where the gold dealers, PWD contractors, and retired military officers lived. Some prosperous journalists and poets lived there, too. The area was always peaceful and without incident. The people who saw Father there said that at that time all he had left on his body were his shorts, the drawstring of which must have been broken, because he repeatedly held them up with his left hand. Another person who saw him there assumed he was crazy. Some others said that he stood in the middle of them and swore loudly all sorts of nonsense. Later, the retired tax collector Soni Saheb and the poet and special correspondent for the city's largest newspaper, Satyendra Thapliyal, both of whom live in that neighborhood, said that they had heard clearly what Father was saying, and in fact he wasn't swearing, he was repeating over and over again: "I am Ram Swarath Prasad, ex school head master...and village head of...village... Bukaylee...!" The poet and columnist Thapliyal Saheb expressed his sadness. At that very moment he had been on his way to Delhi to hear a special musical performance at the American Embassy, therefore he had left the scene in a rush. The tax collector Soni Saheb said, "I felt very sorry for the man, and I scolded the boys as well, but a few of them said that that was the man who had attacked the wife and sister-in-law of Ram Ratan, the gold dealer." He said that when he heard that, he realized that the man could be some good-for-nothing who was putting one over on them. The boys started teasing him, and in the middle of them Father said loudly, "I am Ram Swarath Prasad...ex school headmaster..."

If one were to add it all up, then from the intersection near the Minerva Cinema, where Father got out of the tractor at 10:07 am, to the State Bank on Deshbandhu Street, to the police station by the war memorial, to the Itawari Colony in the northernmost part of the city, all total Father had wandered approximately 30-32 kilometers. These places are not on a line in the same direction. Meaning that Father's mental condition was such that he was incapable of figuring anything out well and he would just suddenly set out in whatever direction. As far as his attack on the gold dealer's wife and sister-in-law is concerned, which Soni Saheb believes, my own inference is that Father must have approached them either to ask for water or to ask where the road to Bukaylee is. He must have had his wits about him for that moment. The women, however, seeing a man in such a state right next to them, must have screamed in fright. The wound that Father received on his right eyebrow, from which blood oozed into his eye, he must have gotten in Itawari Colony, because later, people said that boys stoned him about the body.

Not far from Itawari Colony is where Father was wounded the most. He was surrounded in an open area across from the diner called the National Restaurant. A gang of boys followed him from Itawari Colony, and later some older boys joined them. Suttay, who works at the National Restaurant, said that Father made the mistake of once angrily throwing stones at the crowd. Perhaps a somewhat large stone that Father threw struck the 7-8-year-old boy Vickey Agrawal, who later had to have a number of stitches. Suttay said that after that, the gang became more dangerous. They made a lot of noise and threw stones at Father from all sides. The owner of the diner, the Sikh Sutnam Singh, said that at that time Father had on only a thin loincloth, the bones of his thin body, and the white hair of his chest were visible, his stomach was contracted, he was smeared with dirt and filth, the white hair on his head was all dishevelled, and blood was flowing from cuts over his right eye and on his lower lip. With grief and regret Sutnam Singh said, "How was I to know that that man was simple and upright, respectable and trustworthy, and he was in the condition he was in because of the wheels of fate?" The dishwasher Hari said that in the middle of the crowd Father started swearing at them incoherently and throwing rocks at them. "Come on, you bastards...come on, I'll kill every one of you idiots!...you mother..." but I doubt that Father swore like that. We never heard him curse.

Since I knew Father so well, I can say with complete confidence that by now he had thought a number of times that what was happening to him wasn't real. It was a nightmare. Father must have thought that all these incidents were absurd, ridiculous, meaningless. He must have started not believing that they were happening. He had not come from the village to the city, and a tirich had not bitten him. What's more the tirich doesn't even exist; it's merely a figment of the imagination, a superstition. And it's ludicrous to consider drinking the extract of thorn apple seeds and of finding such a plant in an oil presser's field. He must have thought and realized that no reason at all existed for him to go to court. Why did he need to go to court?

I know that Father must have been having the same kind of nightmare I had, long as a tunnel, fascinating, yet terrifying. He and I had a lot in common. By now he must have been thoroughly convinced that everything that was happening was just an illusion. So he must have repeatedly tried to wake out of his dream. If he started talking very loudly or even began swearing, he did so only in a concerted effort to wake himself up by means of those sounds.

According to the workers and the owner of the National Restaurant, Father was badly hurt there. Many bricks and stones struck him in the temples, forehead, back, and other parts of his body. The street's tax collector Mr. Aurora had a 20-22-year old son Sanjoo who struck Father a couple times with an iron rod. Suttay said that anybody with that many wounds would have died.

I am strangely somewhat relieved and able to breathe easier when I consider the fact that at that time Father must not have been able to sense pain. With his great logician's mind and his profundity, he firmly and totally believed that all this was a nightmare, and that when he woke up, everything would be fine again. As soon as he opened his eyes, he'd see Mother sweeping out the courtyard, or my sister and I sleeping on the floor, or a flock of sparrows. It's possible that, meanwhile, he even laughed a little at this utterly weird dream.

If Father had indeed started throwing stones angrily at the boys, then his reasoning must have been that since these stones were only in his dream, they could in no way harm any one. It's also possible that by throwing a stone with his full force he was anxiously waiting for it to smash a boy's forehead, and suddenly his nightmare would dissolve and the light of the real world would stream in from all sides. Also, his loud screaming was not due to anger, he was actually calling Mother, my little sister, me, or anybody, so that if he were unsuccessful in waking from his dream, we were to come and wake him up.

While the fighting was going on, the greatest irony of all occurred. The head of the village council and Father's boyhood friend Pundit

Kundhaee Ram Tiwari was going down that street in a rickshaw, across from the National Restaurant, at about 3:30 pm. He had to return to the village by bus from the next intersection. He saw the crowd that had formed in front of the diner, and he also realized that someone was being beaten there. He thought of going over to find out what the problem was. He even had the rickshaw wallah stop. But when he asked about it, someone told him that a Pakistani spy had been captured who had been about to poison the water supply, and the people were beating him up. Just at that moment the bus appeared, and Pundit Tiwari ordered the rickshaw wallah to take him as quickly as possible to the next crossing. That was the last bus that would go to the village. If the bus had come two or three minutes later, he certainly would have gone over and recognized Father. That state-run bus always came a half-an-hour to forty-five minutes late, but that day, by chance, it arrived exactly on time.

Sutnam Singh said that the crowd in front of the National Restaurant dispersed when Father didn't get up off the ground for a while. A large brick had struck his temple. Blood had started coming from his mouth. His head was badly wounded. Sutnam said that when Father didn't budge, one of the boys said that it looked like he was dead. When Father still hadn't budged ten or fifteen minutes after the crowd had dispersed, then Sutnam Singh asked Suttay to sprinkle some water on his face, because if he were only unconscious, then he would wake up. Suttay, however, was afraid of the police coming. Later, Sutnam Singh himself poured a whole bucket of water on Father's head. Because he tossed it from such a distance, not water, but mud covered Father's body.

Sutnam Singh and Suttay both said that Father lay right there till about 5:00 pm. The police hadn't come yet. Sutnam thought that he might become forced to be an arbitrator or witness in the affair, so he closed the place and went to the Delight Cinema to see the film.

On one of the streets in the Civil Lines neighborhood the cobblers' shops are all in a line, and at about 6:00 pm Father thrust his head in Ganeshwa's shop: by then Father was even without his loincloth, and he crawled along on his knees like some quadruped. Mud and filth covered his body, and he was cut and bruised all over.

Ganeshwa is the cobbler for the area that is on the other shore of the lake from our village. He said that he was very scared and couldn't recognize Master Saheb. His face was frightening. Ganeshwa got away from him and called for help. Besides cobblers, other people, too, gathered there. When they went inside, they saw Father in the innermost corner of the shop buried in a pile of torn shoes, pieces of leather, rubber, and rags. He was still breathing a little. They pulled him out of there onto the sidewalk. Then Ganeshwa recognized him. Ganeshwa said that he spoke into Father's ear, but Father wasn't able to speak. Much later he said something like "Ram Swarath Prasad" and "Bukaylee", and then he fell silent.

Father's death occurred at approximately 6:15 pm. The date was May 17, 1972. Approximately twenty-four hours before, the tirich had bitten him in the jungle. Twenty-four hours earlier could Father have predicted these events and his death?

The police put Father's corpse in the city morgue. The post mortem revealed that his bones had been fractured in many places, his right eye had been completely smashed, and his collar bone had broken. His death had been caused by blows to the head and an extreme loss of blood. According to the report, his gastro-intestinal tract was empty. This means that the vomiting had gotten rid of the extract of thorn apple seeds.

Thanu maintains that it's now been definitely proven that no one can survive the venom of the tirich. Exactly twenty-four hours later it displayed its amazing power, and Father died. Pundit Ram Avatar concurs. It's possible that Pundit Ram Avatar does so because he wants to make himself believe that the thorn apple extract had no connection at all with Father's death.

I think, that is my guess is, that when Ganeshwa spoke loudly in Father's ear outside the shop, Father must have awoken from his dream. He must have seen Mother, my little sister, and me, then he probably took a twig for brushing his teeth and went to the river. He washed his face with the cold river water, gargled, and forgot all about that long nightmare. He must have thought about going to the courthouse. He was worried about saving our house.

But I want to tell you about my recurrent dream. It goes like this. Via the fields' boundary path and the village's footpath, I arrive in the jungle. I look at the dancing creek and the acacia tree. The brown rock is there where it remains covered by the creek throughout the rainy season. I see the dead body of the tirich on top of it. A sudden happiness surrounds me. Finally, it's been killed. I start pulverizing the tirich with a stone. Thanu stands next to me with the kerosene and matches. Then I suddenly realize I'm not on that stone, Thanu, too, isn't there, and there's no jungle. I'm in the city. My clothes are dirty and have been ripped into rags. My cheekbones are exposed, my hair is all dishevelled. I'm thirsty and I try to speak. I want to ask the way home, to Bukaylee, then noise arises all around me, bells start ringing, thousands of them.

I run away. My whole body seems very weak, I can't breathe. I take some quick steps close together and then make long leaps. I attempt to fly, but it looks like a crowd is about to surround me. An unusual, hot, heavy wind stupefies me. The breath of my death begins to touch me. And finally, the moment comes when my life is about to end.

I weep, try to run away. My whole body, though asleep, is soaked in sweat. I yell in an effort to wake myself up. I try to believe that this is just a dream, and as soon as my eyes open, everything will be alright. In my dream I open my eyes wide and look in the distance. But that moment finally comes.

From outside, Mother sees me. She strokes my forehead and tucks me in with the quilt, and I'm left there all alone. I struggle not to die. I grow weak, I weep, scream, and flee.

Mother says that I still have the habit of mumbling and shouting in my sleep. But I want to ask, and this question has always bothered me, why don't I dream anymore about the tirich?

The Wall

There were five or six of them. For the past twenty years they've agreed on almost every controversial topic and issue of the day. They sign documents as if with one hand. They each express the same opinions about people. If one of them breaks off with someone, they all do.

In speaking, they all make the same mistakes. If one of them stops mid-sentence, another one finishes it. If one of them enters a building, the rest of them do, too. There is nothing–no institution, no funeral march, no book–in which one of them exists without the others. They agree on everything, from how to dot an i, to society and god. Once, I went to a conference where one of them was reading a paper. His paper contained many mistakes, in both form and content. Besides that, it included errors of pure fact, and it used wrong data.

When he finished reading his paper, I questioned him about these errors. For example, the word sarafat is pronounced with a sh sound, as in the word "sugar", not a sound as in the word "soap". The poet Kabir was not born in 1955. The word vicar is pronounced with a short i, not a long one. Ghalib did not die in December, 1990. Et cetera.

Giving one rationale after another, he began justifying his statements. Then I noticed the others slowly gathered around him, and they started to confront me all together.

What happens next is fantasy.

When I argued that his paper was faulty because he repeatedly made mention of bat's eggs, when the truth of the matter is that since bats are mammals, they don't produce eggs, then all five or six of them suddenly started speaking in unison.

Then they turned into bricks. Their heads, hands, feet, hair, torsos, every part of them each turned into a brick, and that pile of bricks formed into a unified, solid mass.

Only many years later did I realize that I had been standing alone in front of an ancient wall arguing with it in a loud voice about its errors in both form and content.

Before people began to doubt my mental health or a brick fell on my head, I got away from there.

And my advice to you is that you, too, be quiet and hightail it away from there.

One Day in The Life of The Indian Ivan Denisovich

For the past six years he wore the same coat. Like leaves, it was a deep green, and very thin yellow veins ran through it. Those veins seemed alive, and when no emotion appeared on his face, their stagger, filth and sadness could indicate his state.

His eyes were small and restless, he often used them to give the impression of smiling. He was bald. His head was round but here and there asymmetrical, like a gourd, and with that shiny dome he could appear good-natured. His belly was flabby and stuck out. The waistband of his pants always slipped down below his waist. He weighed between 100 and 110 kilograms.

His name was not Ivan Denisovich.

He had been born in Meerut and for the past twenty-five years lived in Delhi. Thousands of people were similar, in that they had been born in Meerut but now lived in Delhi, Calcutta or someplace else. They no longer lived in Meerut. But that situation doesn't apply to Meerut alone.

He was an Indian. In the caste column he always wrote "kayastha". He was a Hindu. His father had been the official writer of requests for the sub-district. That was the hereditary profession of kayasthas. For twenty-five years now he, his father's son, was working in Delhi. He had not heard anything about any novel by Solzhenitsyn. So he didn't know anything about Ivan Denisovich either.

His name was Ram Sahai Srivastav. In the area of South Delhi called Ber Sarai he rented a room ten feet by twelve feet. Twenty-five years ago he lived alone in that room, so it seemed huge. But after twenty-five years had passed, six people lived there, so now it seemed very small. It was his family who were responsible for the shrinkage.

His family consisted of the following: a wife who was like a sick, very old, irritable cow; three sons, of whom the middle one was unable to speak and whose left side was paralyzed; the youngest son, who was always sick and suffered chronic dysentery; and a daughter, born in the winter two years ago in this very room but who had no teeth yet and was still unable to crawl. His daughter's legs and arms were all equally thin. She was mostly head and belly, neither of which she was able to lift, so she was always propped up against the wall.

His wife, whose name was Vimala ji, put on clean clothes, powdered her face, made food for everyone, and at seven in the morning went to work as an ayah in a rustic private school. The school was ten kilometers away, and the eldest son went with her: that was where he studied. Since his mother worked there, his fees were forgiven.

Ivan Denisovich or Ram Sahai (whichever name you wish to use) was a proofreader in a private press. He got Rs 650 per month. But he was not a salaried employee, he worked for daily wages. Four years ago, after much effort, he got this job, and it could be said that he was content with it, except that every Sunday, since he didn't work, he received no pay.

Twenty-five years ago the rent for this room was Rs. 25. Now he had to pay Rs 200. Outside his room, fixed into the crooked wall, was a faucet. And right there was a drain. There the pots and pans and dishes were cleaned, the clothes were washed, the entire family took their baths, and in the middle of the night, or when they were sick, they urinated in the same spot. It was right next to the door and was always wet. Because of that, the floor of Ivan's room was always wet, and their clothes were musty.

The faucet was brass. It shone just as brightly now as it did twenty-five years ago. It was probably more than twenty-five years old and most likely made in England. Once or twice Ivan had even thought of selling it. Water came out of it twice a day. For two hours in the morning and an hour and a half in the evening. His household had three buckets. One was bronze. It was very strong, and Ivan had brought it with him from Meerut to Delhi. It had been in that room since even before his wife. The other two buckets were plastic. One of them was red and new, and the other, though it was also red, had been bought from a junk dealer last year for Rs 7. It didn't have a handle.

In his house were pots and dishes, two chests, two rope-strung cots and quite a number of other things.

To attend to the necessities of nature they would padlock the room, and the whole family would go out together. The children would carry along glasses of water while the adults made use of old tins, that were slightly larger. The youngest boy, crying, would be carried by his mother, and the middle boy, mute and crippled, would hold onto his father's shoulder and drag himself along. The baby girl would stay propped up against the wall in the room. In a special, secluded place, above the ditch, along the main road, they would all squat together. Ivan discovered that place ten years ago, when he was newly married and his wife was shy. When everyone squatted there together, no place in Delhi had a more domestic air about it.

Ivan Denisovich or Sahai (whichever name you wish to use) thought a lot. The more he thought, the more his body became still. Sometimes he'd become a huge frog and sit for a long time without blinking. His eyes would remain open, he'd focus on something beyond gross reality, and his mind would function like a machine running in suspend mode. Every sound that reached him would transform into a warm stillness, and all his senses would cease to work. But beneath the bald top of his head, the lines drawn on his broad, long forehead would give one the impression that the huge frog immersed in the deepest level of meditation, that is, Ivan Denisovich, was in the grip of some difficulty or apprehension.

One had to prod him to get out of that state. If he was at home when he adopted that posture, his wife would drop her pans on the floor, smack one of the boys or let fly a torrent of crude abuse at sorne invisible enemies in order to bring him back. Despite his poverty, he had a high standard for fundamental attitudes and thought. Loose, crude speech bruised his soul. When he was harmed in that way, his body shook in anger. In his wife and children, too, he wanted to instill the habit of good speech and behavior.

Ivan loved very much to eat pumpkin. Pigeon peas, too. If pumpkin was made, he'd eat one and a half times his usual amount, along with rice. That's why his wife made it only once or twice a month. What Ivan disliked the most was eggplant. So she prepared that frequently, Ivan ate less, and they could make it through the month, although it was difficult. Nobody knew what his wife liked to eat. Perhaps she herself didn't even know, but many times she was seen by Ivan clicking her tongue after buying tamarind. Even for five paise you could get a lot of tamarind, so she would even use it in the lentils. Sometimes, at night, when she would sit leaning against Ivan, she would tell him about all the tamarind trees there were on the bank of the river in her village, and on the shore of the pond were mango trees, too. Ivan had seen her eating green mangoes, too. She'd put salt and red pepper on them.

Nothing was left of his wife's body. Her nose stuck way out from her face, and her sharp, protruding cheekbones made her face triangular. If someone were to grab her body and shake it, there's no doubt he would hear her bones rattle. Whenever his wife laughed, Ivan heard that rattling sound. Her eyes used to be very big, but now they were only good for seeing. Her body always crackled like dried-out wood, and the room was full of the smoke and sparks of its burning. Her breasts had dried up. With much difficulty their little girl would raise her heavy head and hunt there for sustenance, then tired and frustrated she'd tear the room apart with her crying. At night, especially, she'd often turn the whole place upside down. Vimala ji would hit her all night and be unable to sleep. She'd often hit the children at school, too. Anyone could see that this woman hadn't slept in years and was consumed by a lamentable attempt to get some sleep.

Ivan Denisovich was now thirty-three years old. Nevertheless, about all his hair had fallen out, and the little bit that was left was white. The hair on his arms and chest, too, was white. Once or twice a month his neck would stiffen up, and to see from side to side he'd have to turn his whole body. It was spondylitis. Whenever his neck stiffened up on him, he would respond with enthusiasm. He would bend his whole torso this way and that, rotate it, bend his neck to each side, and then jerk it up and down, and after four or five days of that, his neck would be all right again. His wife never asked him why he behaved like that. Nor did she ever tell him he should see a doctor. Ivan himself preferred to postpone doctors and hospitals as far as possible into the future.

All the same, Ivan needed a minor operation immediately. Last year a bottle of kerosene broke and bits of glass lodged in his right foot. One piece was stuck below the big toe and just above the sole. Because of it Ivan was no longer able to wear his old leather shoes. Instead, he wore flip-flops, whose thong passed above that spot and didn't press against the glass. Sometimes Ivan wondered if, after he died, anyone would think at all about the relationship he had with that piece of glass. And would anyone try to find that tiny, shiny piece of glass in the ashes of his bones?

But Ivan was involved in trying to get some sort of treatment for his middle boy. It wasn't even exactly a treatment because it didn't cost anything and no pills had to be taken. During the year of the handicapped, and with some foreign assistance, some middle-aged, very fair, fat, shiny women involved in social work opened a place for the education of the handicapped in a fine home about three kilometers away. Ivan had known those women since his childhood because he had seen their pictures on calendars and in magazine advertisements. They had a lot of flesh on their bodies, and their eyes and lips were most unusual. It was difficult to say what they could possibly do with them.

For one hour every morning, from eight to nine, Ivan took his middle boy there. Those women had him do all kinds of exercises, they taught him a speech used by mutes for communicating with non-mute people, and they taught him some woodworking and electrical work. A number of other boys like him came too, without hands, crippled, mute or blind. Within three months he had begun to learn something. One day a young, fat, affected woman there said to Ivan that when his boy got a little older and had learned some more things, he'd be able to get some assistance from the government.

Ivan would bring his middle boy back from the training center, put on his coat and head off to work, from which three nights a week he would return home at seven-thirty and the other three nights at nine. It was the middle boy's responsibility, all day, to look after his younger brother and the baby girl. Despite being mute and crippled, he carried out that responsibility excellently. Of all the boys he was the most serious and intelligent. A number of times Ivan felt that his son knew everything about the world and whenever anything "new" was taught him, deep inside he had a good laugh.

Ivan Denisovich or Ram Sahai (whichever name you wish to use) and his whole family were thus an average Indian family. They had food seven days a week, a roof over their heads, and clothes to cover themselves. The children were going to school, and both the husband and wife were employed. Therefore, Ram Sahai's family did not come below the poverty line. And in this sense his was a model family.

Today was the first day of the New Year. It was incredibly cold. The sun huddled in January's fog and haze. The haze of the New Year. In the history of Delhi, within recent memory, no winter like this had occurred before. At night the temperature went below four degrees Celsius. Everyone knew that in the history of free India it was the first time the Prime Minister had been assassinated, but Ivan and his family knew that in the history of free India it was the first time the winter had been this cold.

His wife, along with the eldest, had already left for school. A few dishes had been left under the faucet. Among them were last night's dishes, which Ivan washed in the morning because nowadays his wife spent the night knitting woolens for the youngest boy and the girl. Even though she knew that, despite this, hair still wouldn't grow on her daughter's head and she still wouldn't have the strength to crawl, and her youngest son would still suffer from chronic dysentery; nevertheless, knitting clothes is a way of protecting one's children, so that was what she did.

Ivan opened the spigot, but no water came. Two buckets were completely empty, and in the bottom of the third, at the most, was enough water for five or six glasses, hardly enough for the children to drink all day.

Ivan's eyes had opened late this morning. The children had stayed awake till late. The little girl cried halfway through the night. His wife's breasts had frustrated her again. Once his daughter wept to sleep, he tried to welcome the New Year by making love with his wife. She was tired and kept falling asleep, and Ivan, trying to make music for himself with her bones, finally became tired and fell asleep himself.

The baby girl lay propped up. Her big, heavy head swayed back and forth in a dream. Very slowly. The middle boy was all ready to go to the training center, and he wiped the youngest boy again and again with a rag. The diarrhea of the youngest was very bad today. There was no water. There wasn't even any water for Ivan to take with him to use in the family's secluded spot. His tin can was empty. If the water had come, his wife, first thing in the morning, would have filled all the buckets, cans, glasses, bottles and pots.

Ivan thought he'd make tea. For the middle boy, too. A soft darkness filled the room. Soft enough that everything in the room shone just with its own light. The sun was in the clouds and haze. A sixty-watt bulb hung in the room, but Ivan noticed the switch had already been turned on and the bulb wasn't shining. That meant no electricity today. Ivan touched the electric hotplate, and his mute son immediately let out a terrifying sound and quickly shook his own hand, like someone reciting a mantra. It was the compassionate sound of a deep catechu color that sprang up out of the room's darkness. Next to the hotplate lay its plug.

Ivan noticed the plug must have gotten stuck in the hotplate because its blades were in the receptacle and just its tin handle lay on the ground. He looked in the corner and saw it was empty. His wife usually made rotis in the morning and put them there. What will the middle one eat, thought Ivan. He always got very hungry and ate a lot, and when his hunger got very bad, his entire body shook, as if with fever.

Ivan told his middle boy it was time to go and started looking for the padlock. But the room was dark, and the padlock wasn't in its usual place. The middle boy had dragged himself out of the room, and holding onto the door, was trying to stand up. This was a game of his that he often played when he was alone. When with the support of the door he could stand fully erect, he'd let out a gon-gon sound, jump up and try to run. He could take seven or eight steps quickly in one go before he fell. But that wasn't the end. He had also developed three or four special styles of falling. If he succeeded in falling in the most difficult manner, he laughed in the way that only he could laugh. It was only because of his useless left arm and leg that he was able to play such a game, so he was proud of his achievement. This was a game his elder brother couldn't play.

Ivan, though, couldn't find the padlock. He moved all the dishes and bowls set up against the wall and looked around them. He looked in the space between the joints in the back of his wife's tin matrimonial chest. He looked on the cot where his little girl lay sleeping, and he swept his hands over the top and underneath the bedding. He looked in the buckets. He searched in the niche in the wall where his wife kept her comb, mirror, powder, bindis and knitting needles. All he found there was a fifty-paisa coin that he put in his pocket. He turned over his shoes that he could no longer wear because of the glass in his foot and that he kept under his cot. All that came out of them, besides dust, was his eldest son's marbles and a big brown spider that scuttled away on the floor.

It was getting late. His stomach was growling. There being no water, he had been unable to go out near the ditch and relieve himself. Uneasiness, irritability and anger started creeping through the veins of his brain. Outside, his middle boy was falling down again and again and going gon-gon. The sounds he made went straight into Ivan's brain.

Just then Ivan's foot knocked against the padlock. It was on the floor, underneath the rag the middle boy had used to wipe the youngest. Ivan locked the padlock to the door. The little girl was still inside, lying on the cot, propped up against the wall, her large head swaying to her dream. Even if she hadn't been asleep, she still wouldn't have objected because she was used to being locked in the room every morning for an hour and a half. The youngest son was also accustomed to this routine.

The padlock had been hard to find only because of the rag the middle boy had tossed on the floor. And all the while, the middle boy was engrossed in his game. Watching him fall down, Ivan scolded him harshly, "That's right, haraami, break the other arm and leg..." The boy became scared, and when he fell down this time, he didn't let out a sound. He fell with a dhapp sound, like a sandbag, and suppressed the sound that was about to come out by squeezing his lips together. Then he started crawling toward the wall. Ivan grabbed his arm and lifted him up. Haltingly, the middle boy began to move with Ivan's help and came out onto the steet.

The bus stop was crowded. That meant the bus hadn't come for a long time. And even if the bus came now, so many people would be getting on that it would be difficult for the boy.

Ivan's temples were throbbing. In his ears he could feel the warm sound of the beating of his heart. He could hear it. His stomach was upset. Suddenly, he sensed a slight pain in his neck. It was the familiar pain of spondylitis.That is, the first indication of the inevitable stiffness. He knew that by the time he returned home after proof-reading at the press all day, his neck would be as stiff as wood, and for the next week or so, in order to look left or right, he'd have to put up with a terrible pain. When he was a boy and would get hurt, he used to think how wonderful it would be if our bodies were made entirely of iron, but after spondylitis Ivan felt that things such as iron, stone or wood, which were very hard and strong and which couldn't be bent time and time again like a man's neck or wrists, must be experiencing a great deal of pain inside. Perhaps it was because of this pain that they seemed so solid and lifeless.

It was eight o'clock. They had already waited more than twenty minutes and still no sign of a bus. And today there was a lot of work at the office. The newspaper printed at that press was bringing out today its "Election Results Special Edition". The winning party had

had a victory of historical proportions. Eight extra pages had to be printed. Ever since the election had been called, the weight of the galleys on Ivan's head had gotten heavier and heavier. He had to make it to the office today.

At quarter after eight the bus came. It was already so crammed that people just grabbed onto the handrail and swayed on the footboard like bats. Ivan had heard that bats defecated through their mouths. He was astonished to see that more than half the people at the bus stop squeezed into that crowded bus and disappeared. With the boy, it was difficult to get on. Ivan let it go.

It was the third bus Ivan was able to get on along with his middle son. It was more than half empty. When Ivan Denisovich or Ram Sahai (whichever name you wish to use) got off the bus with his middle son at the stop near the training center, it was already ten minutes after 8:30. Firmly, Ivan said to his son he was to tell the madame he had to leave in half an hour.

But a large brass padlock was on the gate of the training center. It was closed today, and the fair, fat, middle-aged women were nowhere to be seen. A pebble stung the sole of his foot; the thong of his flip-flops touched the glass in his foot and reawakened it. Ivan's face went cockeyed because of those little accidents. He should have guessed that morning that the training center would have been closed today. The sixty paise bus fare he'd wasted.

The middle boy put a finger in his mouth and went gill-gill. He was hungry. Usually he would have eaten four rotis by now. Ivan had in his pockets one rupee and thirty paise. And he had to take the boy back home and go to the office. His wife had gone off angrily today, with the empty bellies of the three children left behind. Ivan Denisovich was feeling faint.

Ivan was angry at his wife. When she knew the hotplate was broken and no food had been made, couldn't she have left a couple more rupees for him? What was he going to feed the middle boy, the youngest boy and the girl? Getting the blades of the plug out of the hotplate would cost another rupee or a rupee and a half. All she ever gave him was just enough for the bus fare. Yet Ivan smoked biris.

In ten years his wife never asked him where he got the biris from or how he was able sometimes to bring the kids toffee.

Ivan Denisovich, who was an ordinary Indian, and who had never heard anything about any story by Aleksander Solzhenitsyn, was pulling out his hair. Making his eyes red, he glared at his middle boy, which meant: "Please don't bother me now, haraami. Leave me alone. Where am I going to get something to feed you? If I don't make it to the press today, the foreman or the in-charge will sack me. You don't know that this is the first day of the New Year and one party has a large majority. Be patient a little."

Ivan decided that tonight, when he came back from work, he would explain to his wife seriously and firmly that if he had a few rupees more in his pocket, he'd be able to make it to work no matter what. Suppose someday an accident happened and he had to go to the emergency ward of a hospital, he should have at least enough for autorickshaw fare. Because when there's been an accident, a man usually isn't able to go to the hospital by bus. He decided he'd say to his wife she should picture him lying on the side of the road, his leg broken and blood all over, and she should feel some compassion. He was hoping to extract some liquid substance out of his wife's wooden, lifeless face. But that hope was negated by an equal amount of hopelessness.

That sickly, old, skinny, wooden woman, whose body was now but skin and bones, whose terrible sorcery, in ten years, had six stomachs to hurl food down into, who was locked in a fierce struggle to get just one good night's sleep, whose quarrelsome and irritable nature was a firm and fierce obstacle to the daily calamities that fell on Ivan's whole family–that woman was now sitting on the most sensitive nerve in Ivan Denisovich's brain and sticking pins into it, and she was hurling the most wicked, vile curses at her baby girl and hitting the girl's heavy head over and over again with her fists. Tears welled up in the eyes of Ivan Denisovich, and he started shaking with pain. The pain in his neck was getting worse, his stomach was growling, and his head started aching. Flames were coming out of his forehead, and his middle boy was sticking his finger in his mouth and going gill-gill, which meant he was hungry.

As if he were trying to scare away a ghost, Ivan shouted, "First we'll go home, then I'll see to your roti. Don't make a scene here on the street, or I'll bury you right here and now!" That was probably not meant specifically for his boy but for his boy's hunger, which was taking over his entire crippled body like a fever and shaking it.

His boy started to cry. Bubbles of saliva burst out of his mouth.

The bus stop for returning home was empty. Also empty was the bus that would come, and they would easily find places to sit. His boy kept on crying, the bubbles kept forming, and each one, as it left his mouth, broke in the open air.

Ivan had started thinking. His thinking started in his brain, and gradually, like the hot wind of summer, penetrated every nerve and fibre of his body. He had become a frog, a rather large one, immersed in itself, and thinking in an unknown, invisible language. That rather large frog was leaning against the railing, and it was absolutely still. Its eyes were wide open, like marbles, and if sand or water were thrown into them, their lids still wouldn't close. With one hand he held his boy's arm, and with the other he clutched the coins in his pocket, and all this was stable, inert, like a stone while the whole world was full of commotion and vibration. The wind was blowing, and people were moving up and down the street.

Ivan Denisovich suddenly came to. He realized he had been standing at the bus stop with his son for over an hour, and so far no other person had come, nor had any bus. He had awakened, not out of a sleep, but out of a very painful, tense, fiery unconsciousness that often squeezed him in its paws. His hair, fallen out and white by the age of thirty-three, the hundreds of irregular wrinkles on his forehead, his neck that stiffened with spondylitis, and his sleep, that would burn his eyes with nothing but smoke for nights at a time, were all gifts of that unconsciousness. It consisted of a light bluish-brown darkness in which off-yellow bats floated like blots. In that darkness he would see a number of scenes from his childhood, his wife beating their baby girl in her sleep, bathing even when she had a fever, and sitting while washing the dishes.

Ivan Denisovich or Ram Sahai (whichever name you wish to use) hugged his middle boy to his side and stroked his head to calm him down. His hands were shaking in defeat. But for quite a long time now the boy had been quiet and had stopped going gill-gill. Ivan's condition had frightened him, and for some time that killed his hunger. Though he was unable to speak, he widened his eyes, aimed them at Ivan and swung his right arm around in circles, which meant: "Let's go home quickly. The little one will be soaked in his own diarrhea by now, and the girl will have woken up and will be crying for milk."

Ivan understood what his boy said without speaking, and he became uneasy. But the bus, there was no sign of it. Across the way came marching in double time a gray-haired old man in white shorts, white shoes, a white undershirt, and carrying a walking stick. He lived in one of the stately homes nearby, had been an important official, was now retired and saw Ivan there every morning as he ran by.

Seeing Ivan, he stopped. In Delhi, seeing someone that much constitutes a very close acquaintance. The old man shook his stick. Because of his running he was out of breath and panting. His stick, too, was panting. The old man said to Ivan, "The bus won't come this way today; The route's closed. The new PM's giving an address today at the Boat Club, so the buses coming from that side have been held up. The traffic will open up again after twelve." The old man smiled and then marched off double time, left-right left-right. Ivan felt the old man was running toward the past, and when he got there in his white clothes and stick, he'd disappear. He felt sorry for him. Because of the direction he was running it seemed he wanted to scare away his own death, who was sitting, waiting for him, somewhere in the future. His running was a painful, but useless, resistance against death.

The strength of Ivan Denisovich's entire body was spent, and the weak emptiness that took its place within him began to be filled with love for his middle boy, for his boy's hunger and his way of speaking. But in front of him was only darkness; he could see no way out. In his pocket he had only one rupee and thirty paise. This was the first day of the New Year, but it differed little from the other days in Ivan's life. Since it was the first day, however, Ivan felt he had to spend all his energy fighting it.

The bus wasn't coming. With the boy it was impossible to walk the three kilometers all the way home. An autorickshaw couldn't be hired. No question about it. With Ivan was his middle boy, his partly-paralyzed and mute son, whom hunger struck like a fever and whose entire body shook like a dry leaf. In Ivan's mind, too, at this time, was his home, three kilometers away, where his youngest son by now was covered in his own diarrhea, and his baby girl's large, heavy head, covered with sweat, was rolling back and forth. She was screaming, because she was hungry. Since her stick-like arms and legs were unable to lift her head and torso, she had only her voice to help her.

Ivan became afraid and uneasy.

Directly across from the bus stop where Ivan Denisovich was standing with his middle boy was a public hospital. A Primary Health Centre. The hospital was quiet. There was no line of patients. The people in front of the hospital obviously worked there. Maybe it was a hospital just for healthy people. Or perhaps because it was small and local it wasn't well-known, or sick people didn't trust it. The only thing certain was that it was there. Across the street, right opposite the bus stop.

Ivan held his boy by the arm and started crossing the street. Jerked along, the boy swung from his father's shoulder and made his way. He didn't understand what was happening, but he had the feeling his father, that is, Ivan Denisovich, had had an idea. In his enthusiasm and eagerness he was going gon-gon. It was like the soft, hypnotic sound cats make when they're petted. Ivan stroked his son's head again, tears filled his eyes and he said, "Sit here, son. Here, in the shade of the tree." The spot was opposite the hospital gate. There the boy sat.

Ivan spent sixty paise on fifty grams of roasted peanuts and seventy paise on a piece of peanut brittle. He put them down in front of his son and went inside the hospital. His pockets now were completely empty.

Sitting opposite the hospital gate like some beggar boy, the middle son of Ivan Denisovich ate his first peanuts of the New Year.

The doctor gave Ivan a form to fill out and asked, "Did you come all by yourself, on your own, or did somebody bring you?" Ivan said he had come on his own. The doctor said, "The rule is that whoever brings a man in gets a twenty rupee commission." Ivan asked the doctor, "Could I put my son's name down for that?" The doctor smiled sympathetically and wagged his head. Nevertheless, Ivan was unable to say "You're very kind, thank you." He remained silent.

The table on which Ivan was to lie down was dirty and covered with dust. The attendant, after settling on a fee of five rupees for the service, cleaned it off and helped Ivan Denisovich lie down.

Ivan experienced no great discomfort or pain at all. It was all over in fifteen minutes. A girl had come to see the doctor, so he had wanted to finish the operation as quickly as possible. Ivan had been scared, too, because once, in his haste, instead of the stitcher the doctor had picked up a pair of scissors. The doctor was young and extremely handsome. His hair and moustache were like those of the gods. The clothes he wore were very clean and expensive.

"Don't you ever take a bath?" asked the doctor. Ivan replied, "When do I get the time for that, sir?" and he smiled. The doctor smiled, too, looked through the window at the girl sitting outside and said, "Yes, you're absolutely right. Where does the time go these days? Anyway, there you are. Your operation went very smoothly. With some patients there's a lot of trouble." Then, as he was about to leave the room he said, "Just be a little careful for a week. Don't do any heavy work, like lifting, and you'll be just fine."

With the help of the attendant and the doctor, Ivan Denisovich got up off the table. He felt weak. Where he had been cut he felt a slight throbbing sensation and pain. Since he hadn't been able to relieve himself yet that morning, his stomach was in knots and burning. His head ached. It was almost eleven o'clock, and he was already late for the office.

The doctor said, "Go to the counter on the first floor. Show them this paper and get your money and a blanket. If you don't need the blanket, you'll get sixty rupees more." When Ivan took the paper and was about to go, the doctor told the attendant to give the patient the food and medicine. So the attendant brought Ivan two boiled eggs, two bananas and a glass of milk. Ivan put the eggs and bananas in his coat pocket and drank down the milk.

The milk smelled strongly of chlorine, and it had been watered down a lot. The glass was ·plastic, and its original blue color had turned a dirty white. When the milk hit his stomach, it knotted up even tighter, and Ivan felt a little nauseous. His headache became worse. In a paper envelope the attendant gave him some pills. For the whole week.

The attendant went with Ivan to the counter on the first floor. He needed to get his five rupees. No one was behind the counter. Climbing the stairs had aggravated Ivan's pain, and his stomach was still deciding if it could digest the hospital's milk. Ivan was worried about his boy sitting alone outside the hospital. Ivan sat on the bench and with much difficulty opened his eyes and looked all around him. The attendant looked at him and said he'd go look for the counterwallah babu and bring him as soon as possible. He told Ivan to rest, because he didn't look well.

Ivan's eyes closed. He was again in the clutches of that familiar unconsciousness: the light blue darkness in which yellow dots floated around. Ivan saw himself standing in their field in the village, with food he had brought for his father, and before eating, with his thin towel, his father was wiping the sweat off his face and arms. Then Ivan saw the village school where he had studied, but just then his wife came and began beating their little girl, hurling wicked, vile curses at her. Ivan's face twisted with pain. His middle boy, sitting outside opposite the hospital gate, suddenly appeared opening the last of his peanuts. He cracked open the shell with his teeth, then used his right hand to pulverize the pieces of shell and separate out the nuts. Then Ivan saw his little girl's large head. It kept getting larger and larger, and suddenly, it broke like a balloon.

Ivan was startled. His eyes opened. The attendant had brought the counterwallah babu and was asking Ivan if he wanted the blanket or fifty-four rupees in place of it.

Ivan Denisovich went up to the counter. He put his signature on the documents of receipt. He did not take the blanket. He also got the twenty-rupee commission payment. Even though the counterwallah took ten rupees and the attendant five, Ivan still had in his pocket now more than 50 rupees.

While Ivan Denisovich or Ram Sahai (whichever name you wish to use) was coming down the stairs, he sensed the first stages of that very familiar, painful unconsciousness, and he knew that blue darkness wouldn't be far away. Yellow blots were flying like bats in his direction. Ivan yelled at them to stay away. Sitting below, the doctor and the girl abruptly let go of each other's hands. Ivan's fists were clenched, his face was hard as a rock, sweat had come streaming out on his forehead, and he was breathing heavily.

Ivan Denisovich wanted to push away those yellow bats flying toward him in that blue darkness of unconsciousness. All he could see was his middle son, sitting alone on the ground opposite the gate, with no more peanuts to eat. Ivan pulled as much air as he could into his lungs and held his breath. This was a fierce struggle. He was battling that unconsciousness with all his might.

Holding his breath, Ivan descended a number of steps all at once and quickly ran away from the hospital. The attendant and the doctor both saw him running. They both yelled after him, but Ivan, still holding his breath, had already gone outside the gate. His middle boy had toppled over on the ground there and had fallen asleep, with peanut shells scattered all around him.

Ivan grabbed him by the arm, lifted him up and practically dragged him toward the street, where a free autorickshaw was standing.

Ivan got in first, then he pulled in his son, and then he pulled the two boiled eggs and bananas out of his coat pocket and put them in his son's lap.

Then Ivan Denisovich or Ram Sahai (whichever name you wish to use, now it makes no difference) said, "Let's go", and he let all his breath out at once. Since he had held so much air in his lungs for so long, when he let it all out, it produced a peculiar, painful, pitiful sound of defeat, as if an engine's exhaust valve had suddenly been opened. Such a sound could not have come from a human being. The autorickshaw raced forward. Startled and afraid, the boy looked at Ivan.

Facing Ivan again was that same darkness: a deep blue with yellow blots. He saw himself at the public assembly at the Boat Club, listening to the Prime Minister's speech, and all around, left right above and below, there was loud applause. Continuous applause. Like so many Sten guns. Then he saw his desk covered with galleys upon galleys of the newspaper, and his wife was using them to wipe up the diarrhea of their little boy, swearing all the time. Then he saw the river in his village, utterly peaceful, flowing calmly. No sound at all.

Ram Sahai, in the autorickshaw, was unconscious. The autorickshaw was speeding along. A little while ago all he had said to the driver was "Let's go". The boy was holding the boiled eggs in his right hand, the bananas lay in his lap, and he was excitedly going gon-gon, gill-gill. Bubbles of saliva were coming out of his mouth, and his short, withered left arm was fluttering about like the wing of a maimed bird.

The autorickshaw sped past the lane that turned off toward Ivan's house. It was New Year's Day. A public assembly was at the Boat Club. Ram Sahai, whose name was not Ivan Denisovich, and who was an Indian, lay unconscious in the speeding autorickshaw.

The Professor's Quilt

This incident occurred at a time when, just like today, the terribly famous playwright and painter Vinayak Dattatreya was unemployed and in a sorry state. And as is the nature of some, Vinayak Dattatreya, too, took those days of destitution and starvation to fall in love, get married, and become the father of two whole children.

Those days he lived with his family in an area of Delhi called Ber Sarai, near Jawaharlal Nehru University, in a room ten feet by eight feet, where the owner of the building, Chaudhuri Mangat Ram, used to tie up his two buffalo. In that one room they all ate and slept, and at the drain just outside the doorway they all bathed and in the middle of the night relieved their bladders, etc. Regular calls of nature were satisfied, as they were by seventy per cent of the inhabitants of Delhi, by a family outing in which each person carried his own bottle or jar of water to the side of the street or the courtyard of the Indian Institute of Technology. That Institute, despite its forbidding reputation, has not yet developed a convenient and affordable technological system for dealing hygienically with the naturally produced biological waste products of the average Indian citizen on the threshold of the twenty-first century.

The advent of post-modernism and socialism, etc. was to have occurred in that very atmosphere and environment of the nation's capital, but even today that has yet to happen, and it certainly did not take place then.

Those days the terribly famous playwright and painter Vinayak Dattatreya was a Research Scholar at JNU. He paid the rent, got his family's rations and provided his children milk, clothes, medicine, etc. by doing translations, private tutoring, proof-reading and the like, and it was during this same period that he wrote his notorious and controversial plays, which have been translated into almost every major Indian and foreign language, and because of which today he is a "known entity."

Winter was coming. Delhi's winter is infamous. The former buffalo stall, in which Vinayak Dattatreya lived with his wife and two small children, had no door. Instead, it had a kind of gate, made up of a few thin horizontal and vertical iron bars. Despite covering it with a dhurrie, sheet and his wife's one and only shawl, the wind still blew right in. And the wind was such that, given the snow-covered regions it came from–Shimla, Manali, Himachal, and Lord knows where else–it attacked the Dattatreya family with its sharp, piercing, icy knives and daggers drawn. The biggest problem was that they had only one quilt, in which it was difficult for all four members of the family to huddle; but the money necessary to buy a new quilt was neither in the hands nor the pockets of the terribly famous playwright and painter Vinayak Dattatreya.

He thought, "We need a quilt. This cold is unbearable."

First thing in the morning, as usual, he went to one of the outer corners of the marketplace of Sector Three of R.K. Puram where he sat in Maqsud Mian's quilt and mattress shop and conversed with Mian Saheb about this and that. Maqsud Mian himself was poor, but his heart hadn't become hard. It didn't take him long, therefore, to realize that this talented person, in the top rank of the literary and artistic world, was in fact greatly bothered by Delhi's cold weather and yet lacked the money to have a quilt made up. That was why he kept sitting there and commenting philosophically about all the world's problems.

Maqsud Mian also realized, however, that this man had too much pride and self-respect to accept a quilt free, so he devised a plan.

The next morning when Vinayak Dattatreya arrived at his store, he found Maqsud Mian with a quilt top spread out on his lap. Testing it between his thumb and fingers and investigating it carefully, he said in a solemn and philosophical tone, "Vinayak, bhai, do you see this quilt?"

"Yes, I see it."

"My customers ... are so ignorant. They just buy what's in fashion. Look at this–what a wonderful design. It was made by weavers and needle workers who have plied their craft for generation after generation. Just feel it. The softness and warmth of pure cotton–you feel them both at once."

Testing it with his fingers, Vinayak Dattatreya said, "Really, Maqsud bhai, this is a wonderful quilt top."

Then Maqsud Mian played the trump card of his clever plan. "Vinayak bhai, do you know how much this sells for, complete with filling and quilting?"

Dejectedly, Vinayak Dattatreya said, "Tell me."

"Just forty-five rupees. Three and a half kilos of high-quality cotton, and this quilt, filled, quilted and ready for use, comes to a grand total of just forty-five rupees."

"Ain?" The terribly famous playwright and painter Vinayak Dattatreya's mouth looked like he had the gapes. "Quilts are that inexpensive? How's that possible, Maqsud bhai, when Delhi hardly has sandals or undershirts for that price!"

"See!" Faintly, Maqsud Mian smiled. Then he stated in no ambiguous terms that if such a fine, warm, top-quality quilt could be found anywhere in Delhi for a cheaper price, by Allah, he'd expand his store.

In two hours the quilt was ready, and Vinayak Dattatreya balanced it on his head and started out for his quarters in Ber Sarai. His heart was jumping and flopping around like a tiny rabbit: he'll shock his wife into silence, and his two kids, when they come home from school, he'll scold them and reprimand them for all sorts of things and then tell them that their punishment was to lie warm and snug in...this! Enjoy, kids.

When he reached the former buffalo stall, now his place of residence, the hair and clothes of Vinayak Dattatreya were covered with wads of cotton that had come out along with the quilt's stitching, and he found presiding there Dr. Prawar Karkat. His wife had given him tea, which he was drinking, and a savory biscuit, which he was just then chewing.

"What a beautiful quilt! It must have been very expensive," said Acharya Karkat, who saw it before Vinayak Dattatreya's wife did and so was shocked first.

Responding truthfully, Vinayak Dattatreya said, "No, sir, it was only forty-five rupees."

"Ain!?" Astonished, Acharya Karkat's mouth puckered and then fell open like a boar's. "I could use one, too. Can you get me one?"

How could he refuse? While he was just as poor and wretched as Maqsud Mian, his heart was big and full of care and concern for his fellow man. Furthermore, Acharya Karkat was a Professor in JNU's Hindi Department, the same department where Vinayak Dattatreya was a Research Scholar; and the Director of Research and Department Head, Professor Kautilya Kesari, was a close friend of Acharya Karkat; and people say that Acharya Karkat got his position there by cooking for and flattering one of the Department's other Professors, Acharya Leela Purushottam; otherwise, his academic record was quite modest compared to that of the terribly famous playwright and painter Vinayak Dattatreya, who was now unemployed, poverty-stricken and residing in a former buffalo stall.

Vinayak Dattatreya immediately promised Acharya Karkat that he would bring a quilt for him tomorrow. He wanted to please Acharya Karkat in every way possible. If the truth be known, however, Vinayak Dattatreya was such a shy and nervous soul that he was unable to please anyone directly. The person he really wanted to please was his Director of Research, Acharya Kautilya Kesari, but only indirectly, through Acharya Karkat. He lived on the hope that when Acharya Karkat would sit in the Department's Staff Room with his good friend Professor Kautilya Kesari, Karkat would mention something or other of a positive nature about him that would bring profound pleasure to the Director of Research and Department Head, Professor Kautilya Kesari. Vinayak Dattatreya had had enough of his straitened circumstances, unemployment, and his family's wretched plight. He needed a job, any job, immediately, so that he could be assured of a steady income and provide his family daal and roti.

However, as everyone knows, they never gave a job to the terribly famous playwright and painter. While Kesari and Karkat both spread vicious rumors about each other and stuck knives in each other's backs, on the topic of giving a position to Vinayak Dattatreya, Bharat and Bhutan or the U.S...and England could not be closer allies. They both said he was a wretched, disreputable, insane, sister-fucker who walked around as if he were a genius; and until they got him on his knees with his nose in the filth of Mehrauli Road, they'd never give him a job.

And, as everyone knows, the terribly famous playwright and painter Vinayak Dattatreya sold peanuts in the street, dealt in second-hand scooters, wrote articles for newspapers and serials for TV, but for a job he never rubbed his nose in a filthy street.

But now–the story of the quilt.

"Here," Acharya Karkat said, "take a fifty," pulling a fifty-rupee note out of his inside jacket pocket and putting it in Vinayak Dattatreya's hand.

When Vinayak Dattatreya gave that fifty-rupee note to Maqsud Mian and asked for another quilt, Maqsud Mian's throat went dry, his heart bent down on its knees, and a jolt of electricity shocked his brain.

Under no circumstances can a quilt be less than Rs. 110. Finding Vinayak Dattatreya to be a virtuous, talented, poverty-stricken and helpless young man, Maqsud Mian had wanted to assist him. Now that same spirit of benevolence was coming back to kick him in the gut.

Maqsud Mian asked Vinayak Dattatreya why he suddenly needed another quilt. Vinayak Dattatreya told him the whole story: Maqsud Mian said, "Vinayak bhai, since this is a matter concerning your employment, I'll have a quilt made for that cockroach that's fallen so low. If it weren't for that, you know what our religion dictates: to touch, even, to look at a pig is an abomination, let alone wrapping one up in a quilt."

The quilt was ready by six o'clock that evening. As much as he could, Maqsud Mian reduced his impending loss. Instead of three and a half kilos of cotton he used only three and a quarter, and half of that was dirty, damp, dead cotton he had taken out of a used quilt. The bottom was made of a thin, cheap "loincloth" cotton used to wrap parcels in the post office. The top cloth was poorly woven and frayed easily.

When the terribly famous playwright and painter Vinayak Dattatreya, with clumps of cotton stuck to his hair, eyebrows, shoulders and face, arrived at the flat of Acharya Karkat, dropped the quilt off his head onto the floor with a bow and raised his eyes, he saw that just then the middle-aged Professor, dressed in a loongi, was engrossed in convincing an uncouth, adolescent-looking student about the importance of "Form and Content" and "Irony and Paradox."

Vinayak Dattatreya's sudden plopping of a quilt on the floor of his flat right in the middle of a profound post-modern discussion struck Acharya Karkat as particularly unforgivable. The student of adolescent and foolish "Form" and wise and clever "Content," covered herself with her chunni, that had been placed on the chair, and quickly put her legs together.

Startled, as if in a "freeze shot," stood Vinayak Dattatreya before them. Below, on the floor, lay the quilt. Despite the fact that Vinayak Dattatreya was a Senior Research Scholar in the Department and the girl was just a first-year M.A. student, neither did Acharya Karkat tell him, too, to sit in a chair, nor did the girl show him any sign of respect at all.

Finding himself in an unwanted and humiliating situation, like a stone in the soup, a bone in the kebab or a lazy man with his hand in the rice, Vinayak Dattatreya said, "So, should I go, sir?"

Just then Acharya Karkat looked carefully at the quilt, unfolded it and spread it out. This thorough investigation, like the final act of a Greek tragedy, proved to be a deep, piercing blow.

"You call this a quilt?...Ain?" From Acharya Karkat's eyes now came not the drunken, reddish glow of passion but glistening yellow sparks of anger.

Suddenly, Acharya Karkat's "Adolescent Form" and "Clever Content" student broke into a laugh. "If you ask me the truth, sir, khi... khi...khi....that's not a quilt, it's package wrap...khi...khi... kkhikhkhee."

Vinayak Dattatreya looked at her with meek, defeated and pain-filled eyes, but that had no effect on her whatsoever.

"I'm tellin' ya the truth, sir, my amma wouldn't even use that as a dish rag. khi...khi...khikhkhee."

Holding up his loongi, and in a peevish tone, Acharya Karkat screamed, "Get this...this...this package wrap out of my sight immediately!"

When the wretched and unemployed Vinayak Dattatreya, disrespected and miserable, again loaded the quilt on his head and was leaving Acharya Karkat's flat, a voice behind him said, "And give the fifty rupees back. Not here, in my office in the Department. Understand?"

Three days later, the second chapter of the terribly famous playwright and painter Vinayak Dattatreya's dissertation, "Ethical Thought in Indian Literature," was harshly criticised by Research Director Acharya Kautilya Kesari and rejected outright.

That year, living in abject poverty in Chaudhuri Mangat Ram's former buffalo stall in Ber Sarai, the terribly famous playwright and painter Vinayak Dattatreya, honored with numerous literary awards, passed the ferocious cold of Delhi's winter in the sublime joy provided him and his family by three quilts. When the Babri Masjid mosque in Ayodhya was torn down by Hindu fanatics, riots followed in India, Bangladesh and Pakistan, and over a thousand Muslims were murdered by Hindus in Bombay, during that entire time, every night, just before going to sleep, snug in their quilts, all four members of the Dattatreya family said, "Thank you, Maqsud bhai, thank you, thank you, a million thank-yous. May God keep you safe."

Even now Vinayak Dattatreya wraps himself up in that same quilt in the winter and spreads it out on the floor to sit on in the summer, and with that quilt as his close companion, he's still providing for his family and writing his controversial and well-known plays.

Tepchoo

What I have written here is not fiction. Sometimes a true story is more amazing than a made-up one. When you've heard all about Tepchoo, I'm sure you'll agree.

I knew Tepchoo extremely well. Our village, Marar, was about a quarter mile from the Son River. Perhaps it was even closer because the village women, before going to the fields in the morning, and after returning from them in the evening, would get their water for use at home from the river. Those women, they never looked tired, and they were always working.

The villagers bathed by dipping themselves over and over again in the Son River. In order to get a useful dip the water had to be deep enough, and for that they would dredge out little trenches for themselves in the riverbed, scooping out the sand with their hands. During the summer the river dried up so much that without such a trench it was impossible to immerse one's trunk. When looked at from our village, you wouldn't be able to imagine how large the Son River got by the time it reached Bihar.

About ten years ago there lived near our village a Muslim called Ubbee. Three or four Muslim families lived on the other side of the leather-workers basti that was on the outskirts of our village. The Muslims raised chickens and goats. The villagers called the Muslims *chikwa or katua.* In addition to eggs and milk, they sold goat meat. They also owned a little land.

Ubbee was a loose, carefree sort of man. He had two wives. Later, one of them, the more beautiful one, started living with the tailor in the market town. Ubbee did not rant or go into a rage. The tailor paid him as much money as the village council demanded. Ubbee used the money to have a good time for a few days, and then he bought a harmonium. Whenever he went to the market, he always stopped at the tailor's house. He had himself a good meal, enjoyed himself immensely, flirted with his former wife and coaxed some money out of her, then bought what he needed and went back home.

People say that Ubbee was handsome. His face had a soft beauty. He was thin. When a child, he was often sick, and later, he was too poor to eat regularly, so his skin had a soft turmeric color. He looked like a white man, a white man who had never been out in the sun. He had the color of wheat that grew in the shade, away from the sun and wind. All the same, I don't know what it was, but he had something that just made the girls go crazy. Perhaps it was because he was always the first to bring the newest fads from the far-away city here to the village: pocket combs, sunglasses; shiny like mirrors on the outside but through which you could see far and wide, yellow basketball jerseys, the bracelet of eight metals worn by Punjabis, rubber whips, etc.

Once Ubbee had his harmonium, he had it wheezing day and night. His pockets were full of books of film songs sold at one anna each. He saw the qawwals in the city, and he wanted nothing more than to become a qawwal himself, but no matter how hard he tried, except for "Hamein toh loot liya milke husn walon ne", he was unable to memorize any other qawwali song.

Later, Ubbee completely shaved off his beard and moustache, and he let his hair grow. He painted his face white with grease paint. The village washerman's boy Jiyawan started going around with him from village to village, singing and playing. Ubbee said what he was doing was "art", but the villagers said he was just an obscene buffoon. Ubbee made enough money to support his wife.

Tepchoo was Ubbee's son.

When Tepchoo was two years old, Ubbee suddenly died.

Ubbee's death, too, occurred in a very unusual manner. It was the early monsoon month of Asharh. The Son was rising. White foam and rotten logs and planks were floating by. The water had become dirty, like the color of tea, and it was carrying downstream rubbish, algae, thatch and grass. That was the flood's advance warning. In one or two hours the Son River would be too high to cross. Ubbee and Jiyawan were in a hurry, so they wanted to make their crossing before the flood. By the time they actually set foot in the river, the water was up to their waists. Where the villagers had scooped out bathing trenches, it had reached chest level. People say Jiyawan and Ubbee were crossing the river confidently. On the opposite bank stood the village women with their pots. Seeing them, Ubbee couldn't restrain himself. Jiyawan struck up the long melody of a *paredesiya* type of folk song. Ubbee provided harmonium. The song was full of sexual innuendo. The women were happy, their smiles beaming. Ubbee became even more uninhibited. The harmonium tied around Jiyawan's neck started swinging out of control. Ubbee took it from him, put it around his own neck and started singing a saucy solo type of folk-song called *salho.* The women standing on the other bank were beaming even more, when screams suddenly pierced their throats. Jiyawan stood speechless. Mistakenly, Ubbee's feet had fallen into a trench or ditch. He went under in the middle of the current. The harmonium strapped around his neck didn't give him a chance to use his arms or legs. Ubbee was just in the middle of imitating a dance Vyjayanthimala did in a film when he went under. Some people say the river also has some quick sand, that they call *chor balu.* It's a layer of sand that looks like it's on the same level as the rest of the riverbed, but once a man steps on it, it lets go into a trough deep enough to swallow a man whole.

Immense efforts were made to find both Ubbee's body and his harmonium. Even the famous boatman Malanga made dive after dive, but it was all useless. Nothing was found.

Ubbee's wife Firoza was young. With Ubbee's death an avalanche of problems fell on her head. She went from house to house to winnow lentils and rice. She started working in the fields. She guarded fields at night for a couple rotis. All day she pounded grain, brought large jugs of water from the Son and had to do all the housework, then at night she went out to guard the fields. At home she had a goat, that she, of course, had to take care of. During all the time she worked, Tepchoo was tied to her belly with an old saree and dangled there like a bat.

Knowing that Firoza was alone, a number of boys from the well-off families tried to get her, but Tepchoo served as his mother's armor. Furthermore, he was disgusting, like dung smeared over Firoza's attractive youth. His hands and legs were thin, dried-out and wrinkly, his belly had ballooned out like a pumpkin, and his body was covered with scabs. Everyone expected Tepchoo to die. A year of incessant labor had gnawed away at Firoza's body. She became old. Her hair was dishevelled, dry and dirty. Her clothes smelled. Her body was greasy with muddy sweat caked over by dust. She kept on working. People began to find her obnoxious.

When Tepchoo became seven or eight years old, the villagers showed some interest in him.

Outside our village, beyond the far-flung paddy fields, was a dense mango grove. It was said that there, in its dark corners, the princesses of the village high-caste farming families, the Thakurs and the Brahmans, would meet their lovers. In one of those same out of the way spots, every three or four years, early in the morning, a newborn would be found abandoned and crying. The great majority of the babies were healthy, beautiful and fair of skin. In no way could it be said that they were the offspring of the village's aboriginals, the Kols or the Gonds. Each time, the police came. The superintendent would set up for his investigation in Thakur Sabeb's house. A whole platoon of policemen would have to be fed. Chickens would be ordered in from the village. Liquor would be provided. In the evening they'd chew paan, smile and joke around with the girls before returning to their station. The situation would always be worked out.

The former name for that place was Headman's Grove. Many years ago the village headman was Chaudhari Balkishan Singh, and he was the one who had had the trees planted. His intention was gradually to appropriate for himself that tract of unused government land. Now two hundred to two hundred and fifty mango trees were growing there, but its name had changed. Now people called it Haunted Grove, because the headman Balkishan Singh's ghost lived there. Whenever anyone passed by there at night, his throat tightened up. Once, Balkishan Singh's eldest son, Chaudhari Kishanpal Singh, was passing by there when he heard a woman crying. He followed the sound, looked through the bushes and briar, but saw nothing. All his hair, even the hair on his head, stood on end. The knot of his dhoti fell open, and muttering "Hanuman Hanuman", he ran away.

Since then, the heart-rending sound of a woman moaning or crying could often be heard there. In the daylight people would find animal bones, jawbones and pieces of bangles scattered around. Some of the village good-for-nothings, however, maintained that no ghost or goblin lived in that grove. It was all just a rumor started by the headman's family so they could use the grove for their sexual adventures themselves and not be disturbed.

Once I was part of a wedding party in a neighboring village. At night we were walking back to our village. It must have been midnight. With me were Radhay, Sambharoo and Baldev. Our way went right through the mango grove. We each carried a stick for protection. Suddenly, on one side, we heard the rustling of dry leaves. It sounded like a wild boar was carefreely rooting around and heading in our direction. We stopped, all senses on red alert. It was a summer night, the month of Jeth. The noise suddenly stopped. Silence stretched out over us. We started looking around, frightened to the core. Baldev stepped forward, "Who are you, bey? Go away!" He struck his stick against the ground, even though he was about to faint. Suppose it's the headman's ghost! Somehow I worked up my courage and shouted, "Hey, bey! Go away!" Seeing Baldev take the initiative, Sambharoo, too, lost his poise. He swayed left and right like a madman. Brandishing his stick, he pounced in the same direction.

Just then a thin, unworried voice was heard. "It's me, uncle, me."

"Who's me, bey?" snapped Baldev.

Emerging out of the darkness came Tepchoo. "It's me, uncle, Tepchoo." He stood like a phantasm in the deepening and lightening darkness of the grove. He had a bag in his hand. Amazed, I said, "What are you doing here so late at night, katua?"

For a while Tepchoo remained silent. Then, afraid, he said,

"Mother got sunstroke. In the afternoon she was guarding the headman's field. She got too much sun. She said she'd get better if she had a drink of unripe mangos. Her fever was really high."

Radhay said, "Weren't you afraid of the ghost, mua? Some day we'll find the bastard's dead body in the bushes."

Tepchoo returned to the village with us. He was quiet the entire way. When we came to the fork of the lane to his house, he said, "Uncle, don't tell the headman, otherwise he'll beat me to a pulp."

Tepchoo then couldn't have been more than seven or eight years old.

Another time it so happened that Tepchoo had a fight with his mother and ran away. Firoza had beaten him with a stick she had just pulled out of the fire. All afternoon, in the simmering heat, Tepchoo wandered through the jungle with the cattle. Then he lay down in the shade of a tree. Tired. His eyes closed.

When he woke up, he felt pangs of hunger. His stomach burned a little. For a long time he just lay there and stared up absently at the sky. When even his earlobes became hot from hunger, he lazily sat up and considered what to do next. He remembered that on the other side of the stand of saraee trees, in the middle of the jungle, was a meadow, and there was Lake Purniha, full of lotuses.

He arrived at the lake. During the day the village buffalo wallowed in its water, and at night wild boar. The water was blackish-green. Its entire surface was covered with lotuses, water-lilies and their leafpads.

A thick layer of algae was in the middle. Tepchoo entered the lake. He wanted to pull out a bunch of lotus seed pods and leaves. Swimming he knew.

Out in the lake he began gathering lotus seed pods. In one hand he snatched up a great many of them. When he turned to go back, he had trouble swimming. The path he was trying to cut through the water was dense with lotus stalks and leaves. One of his legs became entangled in the stalks, and it became more and more difficult to keep his head above water.

When Paramesura arrived at the lake with his buffalo, he heard a goorap goorap sound. He thought it was some huge sunfish cavorting in the lake. In the hot month of Jeth fish sometimes did that to cool off. Paramesura took off his clothes and waded into the water. He dove down where the fish was flapping to grab hold of it by its gills, but what he got instead was Tepchoo's neck. First, he was scared, then he pulled him out. Tepchoo seemed dead. His stomach had swollen up like a balloon, and water was streaming out of his nose and ears. Tepchoo was naked, and the urine was flowing out of him. Paramesura grabbed him by the legs, held him upside down and put a knee in his stomach. With a bhul bhul sound water came out of his mouth.

After throwing up a bucket of water, Tepchoo smiled. He stood up and said, "Uncle, could you pull some lotus seed pods out of the lake for me? I broke off a lot of them, but I lost them all. I'm starving."

Paramesura took the thick stick he used to drive his buffalo and smacked Tepchoo in the butt with it four or five times. Then he swore at him and left.

Outside the village, on the side of the road that went to the market town, was a government nursery. A plantation was being run there. Further in were toddy palms. A lot of villagers were dedicated toddy drinkers, especially the aboriginal laborers who did road work all day long for the PWD. Exhausted from their long and hard labor, they'd get drunk on toddy. First, at evening twilight, they'd secure the toddy bucket high up on the trunk. A toddy palm goes straight up in the air. The only ones who have the courage to climb them are the lizards and the aboriginal laborers. By morning the bucket would be full. They'd climb up and bring it down.

For climbing toddy palms people devised bamboo spikes they fastened to their feet. That reduced a little the danger of falling. If a man fell from that height, his bones wouldn't stand a chance.

Those toddy palms now were legally owned by Kishanpal Singh. The patwari for that area had officially recorded that the land on which those palms grew, even though it was inside the government nursery, belonged to Kishanpal Singh. Now he was in charge of extracting the toddy and selling it. Every evening, in the room where the village council met, and where Mahatma Gandhi's picture hung, toddy was distributed. Inside and outside the room the laborers who drank toddy gathered in great numbers. Kishanpal Singh raked it in.

Once, Tepchoo also wanted to enjoy toddy. He had noticed that when the villagers drank toddy, their eyes filled with bliss. Joy overflowed their faces. Their smiles reached from ear to ear, soft and kind. Floating in bliss and ecstasy, they sang salho and daadar folksongs. They exploded with laughter. They did "intimate" things with each other's sisters and mothers, and no one took offense. It seemed as if they were all swimming together in a fathomless ocean of love.

Tepchoo felt toddy must certainly be a wonderful thing. The problem was how to get a drink of it. Asking the uncles only meant getting a beating, and Tepchoo absolutely hated being beaten. He came up with a plan. The next day, when it was not yet fully morning, when the dawn was just beginning to lighten the sky and a few stars could still be seen here and there, he left the house on the pretext of needing to relieve himself in the bushes.

The height of the toddy palm and the lemon-shaped pot fixed at the top of it didn't scare him at all; in fact, their invisible fingers were calling him up. The palm's undulating fronds, shaking their heads side-to-side in admiration, were describing to him the flavor of their tree's juice. Tepchoo knew that Chapra district's champion stick fighter Madna Singh had been appointed to guard the palms. He also knew that by now Madna Singh would be lying somewhere, snoring off his hangover. Tepchoo didn't feel even a prick of fear.

Like a squirrel, he clung fast to the palm's smooth, straight trunk and began inch worming his way up. On his feet he had neither bamboo spikes nor ropes. He worked his way up with his toes. He saw Madna Singh lying on his angocha beneath a mango tree far away. By now, Tepchoo was quite high. Because of the canopy of the mango, mahue, bahera and teak trees, the trees seemed smaller to him. He thought, "How wonderful it would be if I could fly like a hawk!" He saw a red ant crawling near his elbow, swore at it and continued his climb up toward the toddy pot.

Madna Singh yawned and, rolling back and forth, gave warning that he was about to wake up. The early morning haze, too, was almost gone. Everything had to be finished up quickly. Tepchoo shook the pot. It seemed about a quarter full. He stuck his hand in to better assess the depth…

And that was where everything went wrong.

In the pot was a venomous black hooded snake. A real cobra. It, too, was drunk from the toddy. When Tepchoo's hand came inside, it buried its fangs in it and coiled itself around it. Tepchoo's face went ashen. He tried to fly like a hawk. The palm tree went off in one direction, and parallel with its trunk, Tepchoo fell straight to the ground like a heavy stone. The toddy pot followed behind him.

When Tepchoo hit the ground, there was a dhapp-like sound and what seemed like the final moan of a dying man. Then the pot hit the ground and shattered to pieces. To the side the black cobra lay writhing. Its back had been broken.

Madna Singh came running. When he arrived at the scene, his lungs refused to breathe. He had seen Tepchoo and the pot fall out of the top of the palm tree. He had no chance to try to save him. Once or twice he shook Tepchoo. Then he ran to the village to tell the news of the accident.

Wailing and beating her chest, Firoza went to the spot along with almost the entire village. Madna Singh led her, but once there, he was dumbfounded. It's impossible. This is the same toddy palm. Tepchoo's dead body was right here. It wasn't a hallucination from too much toddy? No, there's the smashed toddy pot. 'And there's the cobra, whose head someone had since smashed in with a stone. But Tepchoo was nowhere to be seen. The villagers searched all around, but Tepchoo Mian had disappeared.

That was the day the villagers became convinced that no matter what, Tepchoo bastard was a jinn, and he'd never die.

Firoza's health became progressively worse. The tendons on both sides of her neck stuck out. Her breasts dried up and hung slack like empty bags. You could count her ribs. Tepchoo she loved immensely. That's why she never remarried.

Tepchoo's antics made Firoza fear he would never amount to more than a vagabond or a bum. So one day she fell at the feet of the village's pundit Bhagawandeen. Pundit Bhagawandeen had two buffaloes, and in addition to some farming, he was in the business of selling watered-down milk. He needed someone to take care of his buffalo, so for fifteen rupees a month and meals, he hired Tepchoo. Bhagawandeen was a real cheat. All Tepchoo got was...one meal a day, and that was only whatever happened to be left over from the night before or some burned corn rotis. Although the agreement was only to have him tend the buffalo, Tepchoo actually had to do everything, in the house, barn and fields. He was awakened at four in the morning, and he wasn't allowed to go to bed before midnight. In just one month Tepchoo's health had gotten so bad that Firoza melted. She burst into tears. She said to him, "Son, forget the pundit. We'll find something somewhere else. This bastard's just a butcher, pure and simple." But Tepchoo refused.

Tepchoo had a plan for this situation, too. After taking the buffalos into the jungle, he'd let them go and finish up his sleep under a tree somewhere. Then he'd get up. He'd bathe the buffalos in the Son river, rinse out his own mouth, etc. Then, after looking around well to see that no one was looking, he'd milk the buffalo into an empty Dalda container and drink up a full kilo of fresh buffalo milk himself. His health improved.

Once, the pundit's wife swore at Tepchoo for something, and to eat she gave him rancid rice. That day Tepchoo had had to weed the pundit's field, and he was beside himself with hunger. No sooner did he put a ball of rice in his mouth than he tasted the acidity and began retching. He dumped all his food in the trough for the buffalo and led them into the jungle.

That evening, when the buffalo were milked, there wasn't even a drop. Pundit Bhagawandeen suspected what had happened, and he beat Tepchoo with his shoes. For a long time he made him squat in the rooster pose. He made him sit against the wall as if he were in a chair. Then he slapped him hard and fired him.

Tepchoo then started working for the PWD. Building roads. Spreading stones, gravel and pebbles. Spreading asphalt. Work for big, big men. Firoza made corn rotis for him in which she mixed spices and salt. During the afternoon break, Tepchoo would eat them and then pour two lotas of water down his throat.

It was amazing that despite such hard labor Tepchoo only became stronger. He filled out. His wrists became thicker, his muscles more defined. Headstrong authority and anger began to glint in his eyes. His hands became as hard as iron.

One day Tepchoo became fully a man. A jawan.

He had cut through the broad stream of sweat, back-breaking labor, hunger, insults, accidents and dangers and had come out on the other side. The grief of despair, dejection or defeat never appeared even as a twinge on his face.

His eyebrows always made clear the presence of one thing–anger, or perhaps the shimmering glint of hate.

Meanwhile, I left the village and took a job in Bailadila at the Iron Ore Mill. Firoza passed away. Baldev, Sambharoo, Radhay and many other villagers also started working at Bailadila. Pundit Bhagawandeen came down with cholera and died. Kishanpal Singh continued his toddy business as usual. For many years he remained the village headman. He built a haveli in the market town, and later, he became an MLA.

Many years passed. I heard no news about Tepchoo, but I knew that in whatever condition he worked, wrung out his blood and rubbed his sinews raw, any other worker would die from the exertion.

I met Tepchoo again when he came to Bailadila. Kishanpal Singh had had his goondas beat him up terribly. Thinking he was dead, they had thrown him into the Son River, but he survived in good shape, and that same night he set fire to Kishanpal Singh's paddy-straw and came to Bailadila. I supported his job application, and he was made a laborer.

That was in 1978.

Our factory was running with the help of Japan. She took almost all the raw iron we produced. The miners were working day and night.

Meanwhile, Tepchoo became one of the guys. They loved him. I had never seen such a straight-forward, fearless, outspoken man. One day he said to me, "Uncle, I always used to fight alone, and I got beat up every time. Now I'm not alone, and with everybody else fighting with me, we'll see how strong the bastards are."

It was about this time that Japan stopped buying our raw iron, and because of that, a government order came to reduce our production. Accompanying that order was a government directive to cut the labor force. The laborers demanded on their part that other arrangements be made for them before the rift went into effect. Paying no attention whatsoever to the workers' demands, the management quickly began implementing the reduction in the labor force. In retaliation the labor union called a strike. All the workers stayed in their shacks. None of them went in to work.

All around, the police were on alert. Some patrols had also been organized, whose job was to sniff out the situation like dogs. Those days I met with Tepchoo on a wooden bench opposite the Sher-e-Punjab Hotel. He smoked biris, wore black shorts and a kurta of homespun cotton.

Seeing me, he smiled and saluted, "Salaam, uncle, red salaam!" Then he laughed, his teeth dark and reddened by catechu and lime, and said, "We've stuck a big fat pole into the management's ass, haven't we. The bastards are writhing in pain, uncle, but they can't seem to work it out. Starving out ten thousand workers while giving the fat cats just a pleasant little tap on the butt is no laughing matter. The downsizing should start from the top. First get rid of Ajmani Saheb, who makes all by himself as much as fifty workers!"

Tepchoo had changed a lot. Behind his laughter crashed the high waves of a sea of scorn, disgust and anger. His chest was visible. The buttons of his kurta were broken. The hair of his chest ruffled inside the throat of his open kurta like thousands of workers sitting outside the high gate of the factory. Tepchoo took a flyer out of the cloth bag hanging from his shoulder, stuffed it into my hand and took off like an arrow.

Three nights later the police raided the union office. Tepchoo was there. With him were a number of other workers. The office was way outside the city, on the other side. No one lived anywhere near it, and on the other side of the office the jungle started, which went on for another ten miles.

The workers stopped the police, but the Superintendent Kareem Bakhs forced his way in with three or four constables. He started gathering files, registers, memos etc. Then Tepchoo pushed aside the officers, came in and yelled, "Darogaji, don't touch any of that paper! My duty today is to guard this office. So I'm telling you. I have no doubts at all about what to do, but you better think about what you're doing, and think hard!"

The Superintendent was stunned. Then, his eyes big and round with anger and his nostrils flaying wide like an ox's, he yelled, "Who the hell's this motherfucker? Tufani Singh, give the bastard ten hard ones!"

Officer Tufani Singh quickly advanced to carry out his orders, but Tepchoo tripped him so unexpectedly that he fell full length on the floor, half outside the door, half inside, like a dead lizard. Police Superintendent Kareem Bakhs looked left and right. His officers were ready, but they were outnumbered. Before he could give the signal, his throat was trapped in Tepchoo's arms.

A gang of workers came in and lathis started flying. The heads of a number of police officers were split open. They cried and begged for mercy. Tepchoo stripped the superintendent naked.

The beateri up platoon of police was marched out. Kareem Bakhs was put in the lead, then Tufani Singh and then all the rest. Behind, a crowd of workers taunted and laughed at them. The police were a miserable sight. The march went all the way from the union office to the gate of the factory, where the workers released them and headed back full of pride and joy. Tepchoo walked tall and sang *salho* and *daadar* folksongs.

The next morning Tepchoo had just gone out of his shack to defecate when the police arrested him. Many others were also grabbed. Arrests were taking place all over.

When Tepchoo was grabbed, he hit Tufani Singh with the lota he used for crapping. It sank into the middle of his forehead, and thick, dark blood came oozing out. Tepchoo tried to run away, but he was surrounded. Enraged, Tufani Singh drummed on him mercilessly, thus accompanying his torrent of curses.

The officers kicked Tepchoo. They beat him with their fists and sticks. Superintendent Kareem Bakhs also got down out of his jeep. He had not forgotten the humiliation he had suffered the day before.

Superintendent Kareem Bakhs told Tufani Singh that Tepchoo should be stripped and a stick should be jammed up his asshole. Tufani Singh delegated that honor to Officer Gajaadhar Sharma.

When Gajaadhar Sharma pulled down Tepchoo's shorts, Superintendent Kareem Bakhs's face went pale. Firoza, according to Muslim custom, had had Tepchoo circumcised. Tepchoo didn't know the Daroga's name, but he knew he was a Muslim just by looking at his face. Daroga Kareem Bakhs whacked him on the temple with his stick and shouted, "What's your name, you motherfucker?"

Tepchoo took off his kurta, threw it aside, and standing as naked as when he was born, he replied, "Allah Baks, son of Abdullah Baks, resident of the village of Marar, in the block of Powndi, sub-district Sohagpur, police division of Jaitharee, occupation–laborer..." and while speaking, he turned around to face Gajaadhar Sharma, who was kneeling on the ground behind him, spread out his legs, and peed on his shoulder, "...district of Shahdol, currently resident of Bailadila..."

Tepchoo was tied up. The rope was fixed to the back of the jeep, and he was dragged behind the speeding and turning jeep for a mile and a half. The road's pebbles and gravel tore the flesh off his back. The flesh of his muscles glistened here and there like red tomatoes.

The jeep stopped at the last checkpoint on the other side of the market town. The faces of the policemen were blazing like bloodthirsty animals. A dhaba was near the checkpoint. They stopped there for tea.

Tepchoo, too, felt an urge for tea. He yelled out, "One tea over here, boy, snappy!" The policemen looked each other in the eyes and smiled. Tepchoo was given a cup of tea. A huge bump had swollen up out of his temple, and his whole body was turning into a cadaver. Here and there his blood stained the road.

About ten miles later the jeep stopped in the middle of the jungle. The area was totally silent. Tepchoo was brought out of the jeep. Gajaadhar Sharma struck him with his stick a couple more times. Superintendent Kareem Bakhs also got out, and he said to Tepchoo, "Allah Baks, alias Tepchoo, I'm giving you ten seconds. The government has ordered that you be expelled from this district. Run as fast as you can down that road. I'll count to ten."

Tepchoo limped and hobbled along. Kareem Bakhs himself counted. "One-two-three-four-five..."

Tepchoo dragged his body along, covered in blood, like an old, sick, crippled ox. He couldn't even stand erect, let alone run away.

Suddenly, the count to ten was over, Tufani Singh aimed and fired first.

The bullet lodged in Tepchoo's lower back, and he fell to the ground like a bag of sand. Some policemen ran up to him. They kicked him in the head. Tepchoo groaned, "Fucking bastards."

Gajaadhar Sharma told the Superintendent, "Saheb, there's a little left yet." Daroga Kareem Bakhs motioned to Tufani Singh. Tufani Singh walked up to Tepchoo, placed the barrel of his revolver two inches below each of his shoulders, and at extremely close range, fired first on the left side and then the right. Even the ground underneath Tepchoo shook.

Tepchoo fluttered softly. Clots of blood and foam came out of his mouth. His tongue rolled out. His eyes turned up and closed. Then he went cold.

His body was tied to the branch of a mahua tree in the jungle and let hang. A photograph was taken. The police reported officially that there had been an armed fight between two rival groups of workers. Tepchoo, alias Allah Bakhs, had been shot and hung. The police had recovered the body.The search was on for the culprits.

Then Tepchoo's body was wrapped in a white sheet, put in a trunk, loaded on to the jeep and taken to the nearest station.

Police detachments came from Raigarh, Bastar, Bhopal and

everywhere. CRP officers went on patrol. Smoke could be seen everywhere. Workers' shacks were burned down. Fifty to a hundred workers were killed. No one knew everything that happened.

In the morning Tepchoo's body was sent to the District Hospital for a postmortem. Dr. Edwin Wargis was in the operating room. He was known for being a very good, pious Christian.

Tepchoo's body was brought in on the gurney. Dr. Wargis observed the condition of the body. In a number of places three-nought-three bullets had entered the body. There wasn't an eighth of an inch over his entire body where an injury hadn't been suffered.

He fixed his mask, then raised his scalpel. He bent down. And then Tepchoo opened his eyes. He groaned softly and said, "Doctor Sabeb, take all these bullets out of me and fix me up. Those bastards tried to kill me."

The scalpel fell out of Dr. Wargis's hand. A shriek came falteringly out of his throat, and he flew out of the operating room.

You're going to say that I've been wasting your time telling you such an unrealistic and impossible tale. You might even say that this whole story is nothing more than a big lie.

In the beginning I submitted to you that this was not a piece of fiction but a true story. Why can't you accept the fact that the reality of life is much more amazing than an imaginary, literary story, especially the reality of the life of a workingman?

Besides the inhabitants of our village Marar, everybody who has ever met Tepchoo believes he'll never die: the bastard's a jinn, that's all there is to it.

If you still don't believe me, then wherever you want, any day you want, and at whatever time you want, I'll introduce you to him.

The Professor's Moan

The professor's flat was right on the outskirts of the campus. Nearby was a grove of lush, green trees. A jungle, and solitude. Utter silence.

At night, after eating, some of the students from the hostel set out for a walk. It must have been about ten-thirty.

From the direction of the professor's place, intermittently, came the sound of someone groaning.

Among the students were some of the professor's favorites. They became worried. Those days many news reports had been printed about domestic servants who strangled or stabbed their bosses and made off with their valuables. Some of them had even been caught.

The students listened intently. They expected the worst. The moaning now became louder and more rapid. Finally, one student worked up his courage. Treading carefully, he approached the professor's flat. Like a lizard, he climbed up the drainpipe to the first floor and reached the window of the room that was full of soft light.

Between the edges of the curtains he looked at the scene inside. He stayed there for quite a while.

What he saw was the professor, who was at least over fifty, making love. The woman with him was the one he had recently selected for the position of Adjunct Professor.

On the professor's buttocks was a boil or wound of some sort, so that when his muscles contracted, instead of pleasure, he experienced an acute, unbearable pain, as if someone had suddenly thrust a long, sharp needle into his body, or a number of scorpions had bitten him at once. That inconceivable, unbearable pain was what he felt each time he tightened his buttock muscles for pleasure, and each time he did that, he moaned.

When the professor's moans became louder and came even more quickly, the student came back down the drainpipe.

Returning to his friends, he gave an exact description of what was going on in the flat. All the students went back to the hostel.

This news gradually spread first among the students of the department and then throughout the entire university. The professor was completely unaware.

Now every night precisely at ten o'clock many groups of students go out for a walk toward the jungle and wait for the moans to rise up out of the professor's flat.

Many times, in fact, the professor moans because of the pain caused by his boil or wound, and that sound sends a wave of indescribable bliss over the students hiding in the bushes in the darkness of night around the professor's flat.

The professor's moan comes out of the building, and the boys put their hands on each other's shoulders and softly whisper, "Stick with it, guruji, stick with it!"

Nailcutter : A Memory Fragment

During the month of Saawan a soft darkness would melt into the green of the grass and trees. The air would become heavy and fluid. The drops of rain would swim in its folds.

I was nine years old.

During that month there was so much fun. Rakhis were tied. Kajlis were sung. For naag panchami the seven sisters were made of cow dung. We filled a leaf basket with paddy and milk and went out looking for the snakes' holes.

The *hariyali amavasya* also occurred during that month when farmers could relax and celebrate their lush, green fields. I made high bamboo stilts, got on them and ran. I would then become at least twelve feet tall.

Mother lived in one of the southern rooms. She had been brought back from Bombay's Tata Memorial Hospital. She only drank pomegranate juice. In order to talk she put her finger in the hole the doctors had made in her throat. There a tube was attachéd. Through that tube she was able to breathe.

Very thin, cold and weak was that voice of hers. Almost like a machine's. Like the very low volume of a radio heard only during huge downpours and the crackling of lightning, or when the tuning needle got stuck between two distant stations.

Speaking must have caused her a lot of pain. She spoke rarely. In that machine-like sound I tried to find her old, genuine voice. Sometimes I heard something that sounded the way Mother's voice used to be. Then she became the same Mother who was in my young memory.

But Mother listened to everything. Everything. When we talked, fought, screamed or called out for each other, Mother listened longingly. Our words must have given her some comfort.

Only her eyes allowed me to hope she wasn't going to go away, that she would stay with me my entire life. I wanted her with me always. Even if she was only like a picture or a statue, even if she never spoke. I still believed she would be alive then; a faith I did not have in pictures.

Sometimes I became very frightened and cried. A very empty, completely empty space would suddenly appear in my life. It was horrifying.

One day Mother called for me. Outside, the grass in the meadow was deep green. The sky was filled with clouds, and the air was heavy and humid.

Mother put out her hand to me. The nail of the finger next to the little finger of her right hand had partially torn. It must have made her feel uneasy.

That finger is called the finger of the sun.

I understood, and brought the nailcutter, and sat on the floor next to her bed. I was to use the file on the nailcutter to file down that nail and make it even. That's what she wanted. That nailcutter father had brought from Allahabad, when he came back from the Kumbhamela, two years ago. It was decorated with a sitar made of blue glass.

Mother's fingers were exceedingly thin. They lacked blood. Her skin was yellowish. It was thin, like kite paper. No, not even yellow; old ivory. And very cold. With a cold that lifeless things have, like chairs, tables, door leaves, bicycle handlebars.

And how had her hand become so light? Where had all its weight gone? Maybe that weight is the weight of life the earth pulls toward itself with its magnet. And now Mother had very little of it left.

I held her hand and slowly rubbed her nail with the file. I wanted to make her nails very beautiful, fresh and shiny.

I laughed. Then I kept on smiling. That was my way of consoling her and making her happy. I noticed how much she was enjoying her nail being filed gently. Her face shone with a happiness that filled her entire body with peace. She closed her eyes.

It took an hour. I didn't do just the torn nail, I fixed up all her nails very nicely. She looked at them. What a moment of weakness and defeat when fingernails give us hope to live. How beautiful and glossy her nails had become.

Mother touched my hair. She wanted to say something. But I stopped her.

If she had spoken, she would have asked why I hadn't taken a full bath, why I hadn't washed my hair, why I was covered in dust, and why I hadn't combed my hair.

That night was cold. The rain was pouring outside. A night rain during Saawan has its own deep sound. As if all the world's winds were blowing around inside a huge pot. As if there was no way to get out.

At five o'clock the next morning, in our courtyard, the women of the village were weeping. Not weeping, grieving. During the night Mother had died in her sleep.

Mother had died.

Never again did I see her filed nails. That night, before going to sleep, I put the nailcutter under my pillow.

Since then, I've often looked for that nailcutter. Even today. Many years later. But I've never found it. I have no idea where it is.

It's possible that it's in a very obvious place and I'm unable to find it only because of my forgetfulness. I often go around looking for it.

Because things never get lost. They stay right where they are. With their complete existence and full weight. We just forget where we put them.

Job Search

This is about those days when Mahapundit Rahul Sankrityayan was unemployed. His wife was ill. He was unable to pay his children's school fees. His financial situation was so bad, in fact, that he was barely able to eat.

Rahul ji, however, had a great amount of self-respect. He never revealed his troubles or worries to anyone.

During that time the newspapers carried an advertisement which stated that the All India Rahul Sankrityayan Research Institute had two openings, for a translator and a book editor.

Since he knew many languages, and since he had a great deal of experience in editing and publishing both his own books and many rare manuscripts, Rahul Sankrityayan applied for both positions.

A month later the All India Rahul Sankrityayan Research Institute sent him a card inviting him for an interview. Since he also received third-class train fare, he was able to go.

In the interview he was asked questions about *From the Volga to the Ganges, An Introduction to Philosophy, Don't Escape, Change the World,* and *A History of Central Asia.* Since Rahul Sankrityayan had written those books himself, he responded in a very matter-of-fact tone, and he often had to correct the mistakes committed by the members of the screening committee.

When he left, the Director of the Research Institute, who was also the chairman of the screening committee, asked the other members of the committee for their opinions about the candidate.

The committee members were in a quandary. Then one of them spoke up. "Sir, the question is one of qualifications and past

The Correct Answer

It was implemented by the President, the Mafia and the Army. Tanks, mortars, the Special Task Force and commandos were brought into the capital. Rocket launchers fired missiles at Parliament House. Hundreds of Members of Parliament were arrested. A State of Emergency was declared throughout the land. Newspapers were censored. The Constitution was abrogated. The country's entire administration ran on the Executive Orders issued periodically by the President. A curfew was imposed in all the large cities. Strikes, demonstrations, marches, speeches, etc. were all declared illegal. Elected panchayats, municipal corporations and regional units were disbanded and their administrative duties were given over to Army Officers and Federal Bureaucrats. The Army and the Police murdered between a thousand and fifteen hundred people, including the elderly, women and children, and this was the official report: "Some dangerous professional criminals were arrested, some were killed, and the Army is leaving no stone unturned in its operation to capture the remaining criminals, wherever they may be hiding." Elections were postponed, and at night the President used the radio and television to address the nation. The essence of his message was this: "We have now removed all the obstacles that have been hindering the development of our economy, commerce and international trade. This is an important lesson of history. We have implemented it."

Having carefully read the above description, in one word tell us what the President has implemented. For the correct answer turn this page upside-down.

Bibliography

Heeralal's Ghost : The Hindi original appears on pp. 123-143 of the collection of short stories entitled *Tirich*, published in 1989 by Vani Prakashan Group. The Hindi film *Uparaant* is based on this story.

The Helper : A Memory Fragment : The Hindi original appears on pp. 29-34 of *Aur Ant Me Prarthana*, published in Panchkula, Haryana, by Adhar Prakashan in 1994.

The Third Degree : It was first published in the journal *Indraprasth Bharati* in 1993. Later, it was published in the journal *Pal-Pratipal.*

The Golden Waistchain : The Hindi original *Chappan Tole Ka Karadhan* appears on pp. 47-67 of the collection of short stories entitled *Tirich*, published in 1989 by Vani Prakashan Group, New Delhi.

Tirich : The Hindi original first appeared in the literary magazine *Hans* in 1988. It was reprinted in 1989 as the primary story in a collection of short stories by Uday Prakash called *Tirich : Uday Prakash ki Nau kahaniyan*. In 1992 it was reprinted in the anthology edited by Rajendra Yadav called *Samkalp : Kathadashak* (Delhi : Hindi Academy). An Urdu translation appeared in late 1996 in the Karachi magazine *Sareer*. This English translation was first published in 1988 in *Pig Iron's* number 15, entitled *Third World.* The present text has been changed slightly.

The Wall : The Hindi original is on pages 47-48 if *Aur ant mein Prarthana,* published by Adhar Prakashan, Panchkula, Hariyana, 1994. Now published by Vani Prakashan Group, New Delhi. This translation was published on pp. 84-85 of *Indian Literature*, the English language literary journal of the Sahitya Akademi, pp. 173 (volume 39, number 3), May-June, 1996.

One Day in The Life of The Indian Ivan Denisovich : The Hindi original appears on pp. 68-88 of the short story collection *Tirich* published in New Delhi by Vani Prakashan Group in 1989.

The Professor's Quilt : The original Hindi text appears on pp. 15-17 of the February 1997 issue of the monthly literary magazine *Hans*, published in Delhi.

Tepchoo : The Hindi original appears on pp. 86-102 of the author's first short story collection *Dariyai Ghora* published in 1982 by Sambhavana Prakashan in Hapur, with illustrations by Sarveshwar Dayal Saxena.

The Professor's Moan : The Hindi original is on pages 56-57 of *Aur ant mein Prarthana*, published by Adhar Prakashan, Panchkula, Hariyana, 1994. Now published by Vani Prakashan Group, New Delhi. This translation was published on pp. 81-82 of *Indian Literature*, the English language literary journal of the Sahitya Akademi, number 173 (volume 39, number 3), May-June, 1996.

Nailcutter : A Memory Fragment : The Hindi original appears on pp. 9-12 of the collection of short stories entitled *Tirich*, first published in 1989 by Vani Prakashan Group, New Delhi.

Job Search : The Hindi original is on pages 56-57 of *Aur ant mein Prarthana*, published by Adhar Prakashan, Panchkula, Hariyana, 1994. Now published by Vani Prakashan Group, New Delhi. This translation was published on pp. 82-84 of *Indian Literature*, the English language journal of the Sahitya Akademi, number 173 (volume 39, number 3), May-June 1996.

The Correct Answer : The Hindi original is on pages 56-57 of *Aur ant mein Prarthana*, published by Adhar Prakashan, Panchkula, Hariyana, 1994. Now published by Vani Prakashan Group, New Delhi.